CHIEF
OF
STATION

J.D. Narramore

This is a work of fiction. All of the characters, organizations and events in this novel are either products of the author's imagination or are used fictitiously.

www.jdnarramore.com

ISBN: 9798664529821

To C. Wayne Allen,

A great storyteller and an even greater Grandpa

CHIEF OF STATION

ACKNOWLEDGMENTS

Special thanks to my cousin, Mitchell Allen, for taking on the task of editing this novel. In the midst of grad school and a full-time job, he provided invaluable feedback and suggestions.

Writing a first book isn't always easy. When I needed it most, my brother Tyler offered both words of support and a creative writing MasterClass to help develop my skillset.

Lastly, not everyone can say their significant other didn't complain when evenings were spent focused on research or writing. My fiancée, Hallie, has been a constant source of encouragement throughout this project.

CHIEF OF STATION

1

The First Day- March 9th, 1983

Yuri Ustinov had always been and would always be, a particular and timely man. Believing in absolute orderliness and attention to detail, he kept everyone he supervised at the Ministry of Railways on their toes. A subordinate arriving but a second late to a meeting with him would suffer a severe verbal lashing. The opposite held true, however, for Ustinov's superiors. Waiting to meet with the Minister himself, his stubby fingers tapped loudly against the wooden armrest of his chair. The secretary seated at her desk across the room was becoming increasingly annoyed with him. At ten minutes past nine, he finally arose somewhat exasperated and approached her. Just when should he expect to see the Minister of Railways, Viktor Molotov? The brusque secretary reluctantly pressed a button on her desk. Immediately a voice came from the intercom.

"Yes Katya?"

"Minister Molotov, Yuri Ustinov is here to see you for your 9 o'clock appointment."

"Tell him unexpected business requires me to postpone our appointment. Please reschedule with him."

The Minister of Railways released his finger off the intercom button, returning his attention back to the conversation with his old friend: Major Pyotr Ivanovich of the KGB.

The Major sat lost in thought as he looked out the near frosted-over windows and onto the heavy snow blanketing Red Square. From the warm comfort of the Minister's office, he could see the Kremlin guards doing their best to cope with the frigid temperatures and icy air blowing hard from the east. If the weather reports were correct, they would find little solace for some time. The same of which, he considered, could be said for the state of their own country.

"Sorry about that Pyotr."

"Oh, you're fine," he replied as he turned back to look across the desk at his old comrade. "Please continue."

"As I was saying, the Central Committee's next meeting is not that far away. The snow will soon melt, spring shall arrive in the *Rodina*, and we'll be faced with the undercurrents of so-called reform. Do not misunderstand me. I'm in full support of our General Secretary. However, I can't help but suspect that some manipulate him now in his advanced years."

"Might it be that those whom you are anxious about are just younger than you and I, Viktor?"

"Young, yes, but also ignorant of what reckless reform can lead to. It was reckless reform that led to Khrushchev's downfall nearly twenty years ago. The younger generation is susceptible to materialistic ideas from the West, as well as such selfish pursuits that would destroy the common good and pave the way for us to be under the boot of the Americans."

Major Ivanovich nodded in agreement. "So we must set an example for them and lead in the way that Brezhnev did."

"That we shall, but it won't be enough. See now, Brezhnev is gone and Andropov is in the autumn of his years. It's within the realm of possibility that we shall soon be faced again with choosing a new leader. What is stopping a younger, charismatic, reform-minded man from winning over the Committee?"

"Chernenko would be the most logical next in line."

Molotov leaned back in his chair and pondered his friend's remark. "That I'm not so sure. He failed to gain enough support when Brezhnev died. He could very well fail again next time around."

"You suppose maybe that young man that used to oversee Stavropol?"

"And now has a seat on the Politburo? Yes Pytor, I most definitely suspect Mikhail Gorbachev could be our next leader," replied Molotov disgustedly. "Andropov shows favor to him. At times he even allows him to chair meetings! As shrewd as that old KGB headmaster is, he's making a mistake. Gorbachev would make irreversible changes that would harm our power and system of rule."

The Major nodded his head in agreement. "Maybe if he had fought in the Great Patriotic War, he would have greater respect for this communist system of ours. It's remarkable that one with such ideas could work their way up The Party ladder as he has."

Molotov's eyes suddenly turned cold and calculated. "Comrade, that is why something must be done. That is why something will be done. And that is why I have asked you to come here today."

"Go on."

"What I am about to say to you is said in the strictest confidence."

"Understood Viktor."

"There is a group of staunch Soviet patriots, like you and I, who wish to prevent this fool from ever taking power. Men on the Central Committee, the upper hierarchy of your own KGB, and even the Politburo. We have formed a pact to work together in seeing that he goes away."

"How so?"

With a stone-faced expression fitting of an executioner, Molotov spoke but a single word. "Permanently."

A deafening silence filled the room. Finally, Ivanovich spoke.

"How can I be of help?"

A smile slowly formed on the old Soviet oligarch's face. "Only with the most important part, comrade. Only the most important part."

***

It was at the end of a long day at the Lubyanka that Ivanovich returned to his apartment shortly after six. Slowly pulling up to the curb of the building where the privileged and ruling class resided, the driver got out and opened Ivanovich's passenger door. The Major nodded his head in quick acknowledgment before making his way inside to where the elevator doors were just then opening. The operator, a small balding man who had four sons currently fighting in Afghanistan, greeted him. "Good evening Major Ivanovich."

"Good evening to you comrade Somov. How is your family?" Ivanovich asked as the doors shut and the elevator made its way to the 6th floor.

"Doing fine, Major. My wife and I received a letter from our youngest today. He's been promoted to sergeant."

Ivanovich recalled a memory but chose to shut it out immediately, lest his emotions show. "Treasure your children comrade. They are the ones who go before us and leave a legacy when we're gone."

"Very true comrade."

The doors opened and Ivanovich proceeded down the hall to his door. Before opening, he attempted to put aside the pressing issue still swirling in his mind. Taking a deep breath, the Major entered to the joy of his family.

"Oh Pyotr! You're home. Come, I've made dinner am just setting it out onto the table," his wife spoke from another room.

The Major took off his overcoat and went to look for his wife. Thirty-six years they had been married. Of those thirty-six years, this was his favorite part of each day. He entered the kitchen to find her picking up two bowls of soup to take into the dining room. "How was your day?" she asked with a welcoming smile.

He gave her a quick kiss. "The usual. More paperwork. How is Fyodor?"

"In his room studying," she said as she went into the dining room to set down the bowls of beet and cabbage red soup known as *Borscht*, looking everything over before deciding dinner was ready. "Fyodor, dinner is ready and your father is home."

Pyotr's teenage son soon entered the room. With his blue jeans and affinity for anything Western, he was a picture of the new generation of Russians. The old guard was losing a war to turn back the tide on its young people's passions as the father could easily see.

As they ate their dinner, the Major sat in silence while his son excitedly explained all he was learning for his upcoming engineering exam. He loved his son whole-heartedly, however, it was all he could do to feign a smile and pretend to show interest. The meeting with Molotov engulfed his thoughts. *How can they ask me, a veteran KGB officer, to become a co-conspirator in a plot to eliminate a member of the Politburo and possibly any hope of saving this country from itself?*

He could see the writing on the wall. The system was built on a foundation of lies that infected nearly every system of the government. Everything from the news of the goings-on in the West to economic reports of the *Rodina* itself—nothing could be trusted. If it really were a 'worker's paradise,' why were there constant food shortages and long-lines for the working class? Change was needed. Change led by one who wouldn't give in to the greybeards and the corrupt.

Lying in bed later that evening while his wife slept beside him, his pressing thoughts remained. Ivanovich turned and reached over for his alarm clock: half-past three. *It's pointless trying to get sleep tonight. I know what needs to be done.*

Rising carefully so as not to wake up his wife, he made his way to the kitchen to find a bottle of *Stolichnaya*. He poured himself a shot of the Soviet-brand vodka and downed it fast. The tense feeling throughout his body eased somewhat as the warmth from the liquid went down. Ivanovich cleared his throat and sighed. He couldn't let this good man get killed. There was but one way to stop it from happening.

Pouring himself several more shots into a glass, the KGB Major walked into the living area and opened a cabinet. Inside were several photograph albums. Reaching for a dusty green one with gold trim on its cover, he carried it over to his favorite chair. His body plopped down into the seat like that of a much older man who had long carried a heavy load. Indeed, he had been carrying a heavy burden now for nearly fifteen years. He opened the album and looked with fondness at the first two photos of a young boy, no more than five, spending the day at a resort by the Black Sea with his parents. Pyotr remembered that time from so long ago before he was in the commanding position he had now—when life seemed simpler and his allegiances more straightforward—when the most precious things to him were his wife and his first-born son, Misha.

He turned to the next page to see his son now ten years old and with the biggest smile on his face—a photo of him on a camping trip out in the woods. Like all Russian parents, Pyotr adored his children. He recalled proudly how outgoing and adventurous Misha was from an early age. The father knew early on that his son would never choose a career behind a desk if he could help it. The son longed to be a hero like those he'd heard about from the war. His mother often caught him in their bedroom, peering inside their dresser drawer at his father's "Order of the Red Star" medal, awarded for bravery at the Battle of Stalingrad.

Ivanovich continued looking fondly at the pictures of his son until coming to one of him in uniform with his newly sewn-on shoulder marks befitting a commissioned officer. A mixture of anger and pain took hold of him.

Misha had been in the army for no more than a year when, in August of '68, he was sent to take part in Operation Danube. In an effort to thwart a Warsaw Pact member nation's reforms and movement towards democracy, the Soviets invaded Czechoslovakia with little warning. In Prague, the young officer received orders to take his tank and provide the support needed for soldiers to storm a radio station that was encouraging resistance. However, Czech citizens barricaded the station with transit buses. As his tank pushed through the barricade, it caught fire and was forced to stop. Several young men rushed towards their armored vehicle and tried to climb on top. One succeeded, and to his luck, the crew had failed to lock the top hatch of the T-62. Misha and his comrades suddenly looked up to see the light from outside and two petrol bombs hurled down. The glass bottles smashed against the floor as flames rushed forth, blanketing all of the men. They frantically attempted to push open the hatch, but to no avail. The Czech outside, along with another compatriot, had succeeded in jamming it shut. By the time help arrived, the human faces were burned beyond recognition, with only Misha still alive.

Pyotr recalled that very last time he ever saw his son. In the hospital room here in Moscow, it was all that he could do to hold back tears in front of Misha. His skin completely burned off; every moment the young man had left was spent in agony. When it was over, the Major's views about everything changed. The lingering questions and concerns he once held were pushed aside. Now, an intense hatred fermented for the strong men pulling the levers in the Kremlin—the very ones he worked alongside for decades and to an extent was one of. For too long, he'd ignored what was plain to him until this loss forced him to open his eyes. Misha had no business being in Czechoslovakia. If the people there chose a different path, let them. Maybe it was time for his own country to try democracy and reform for a change. The system needed to be torn down. He was sure of it. From then on, Pyotr would do whatever possible to make that a reality.

Several months later, he made the fateful decision that had changed everything: he became a spy for the United States.

Was he a traitor to his country? Ivanovich didn't

think so. Just as his son saw him for his service in the war, he saw himself as a patriot, trying to save his country from men who had consolidated power for themselves atop a worker's paradise that never was and never would be.

When he next met with his handler, a young CIA officer in his early thirties, he would tell him all about this plot. Would the Americans do anything to foil this assassination attempt? That was a perplexing question. What he did know, however, was that it would be his best chance to do something without risking exposure. There was no way of knowing who all was involved. If he could make the Americans understand the potential of having a man like Gorbachev as both General Secretary and negotiating partner one day, they'd have to step in.

Ivanovich looked for a moment longer at the last photo taken of his son. "I do this for you Misha," he said softly aloud. Taking the glass of *Stolichnaya*, he emptied it before closing his eyes and finally falling asleep in his chair.

A few hours later, he awoke to the ill effects of his late-night drinking. He knew just the cure. Getting dressed as his wife still slept, he called for his driver and headed downstairs. When he got into the car, the driver immediately noticed the bloodshot eyes and worn look on the Major's face.

Often he would drive Ivanovich like this early in the morning. Unlike so much of Soviet life, however, these trips were unpredictable. Several blocks away from the Kremlin, the car pulled up in front of the

Tenishev Steam Baths. There, others like the Major arrived early to soothe the hangovers that plagued them. Ivanovich entered the building and made his way to the men's steam rooms. Once inside, he undressed in the changing room and took a towel and a handful of birch tree branches. Opening the door that led to the steam rooms, he immediately felt the warm air rush towards him. It was through this sweating out of the poisons that he felt both renewed and mentally refreshed.

There were already several other men inside the *banya* when he entered. Their heads hung low, breathing in deeply and slapping the birch branches against their backs. He recognized some of them, regulars, as he took a seat at the far end away from everyone. He was in no mood to visit.

What exactly would he say to his American handler? The next rendezvous was in four days. He pondered how best to present his intel in the short time they would have.

Soon it was time to go. The Major rose and headed to the showers where the ice-cold water did the final trick in preparing his body for the long day.

"Major, it is good to see you this morning," an overweight man with a round face bellowed as he slapped Ivanovich's bare back. He appeared to still be drunk from the night before, or perhaps he had already started the day with a few drinks. "What brings you here this morning? I believe this is the first time I've seen you here on a Tuesday!"

Ivanovich's mind raced to remember who this man was until the answer came to mind. "Ah, General

Samovich. It is good to see you. I come here every so often. It's good for an aging body like mine."

"Very true, and for an officer of the 2nd Directorate like me, it is best to stay in top shape, lest a capitalist spy gets by me on the streets."

Pompous louse, Pyotr thought to himself. *It's well-known throughout the inner circle of The Party that you only received your position within the KGB because of your wife's uncle, and that you've never exerted yourself any more than when cheating on her with your secretary.*

"I'm afraid I must be going now comrade. Can't be late to the office," he said in a deflective manner as he reached for a towel lying on a nearby cart, hoping to return to his thoughts and escape from this idiot.

General Samovich missed the visible social cue. The KGB officer leaned in towards the Major, revealing the liquor on his breath. "Comrade," he spoke in a slightly lower but still easy to hear voice. "I must congratulate you for taking a role in defending our *Rodina*."

"I do not understand…"

"You know! Our plan to put away that fool whose ideas are as bad as Khrushchev."

Ivanovich's heartbeat nearly stopped at the sound of this man's loose words. *He must be out of his mind drunk. What if someone should hear what he's saying? Someone loyal to The Party would implicate me to all of this in an instant!*

"Comrade, I don't think…"

"You are not the only brave Soviet who has taken

a stand," he said as he raised a fist in the air. "There are others such as…"

Ivanovich's eyes began to dart around, looking for any sign of someone that could be watching. Part of him instinctively desired to run away lest he be seen with this drunken KGB General who was foolishly speaking out loud, not just of his own role in an assassination plot of a member of the Politburo, but the names of his fellow conspirators too. The Major's brain overrode these instincts by telling himself just how valuable this intel was.

"Now comrade, please be careful who you tell," he said as if the effects of the booze had worn off momentarily. "We must exercise caution or our very lives could be at risk."

Ivanovich briskly nodded. With that, Samovich smiled and went on his way towards his own locker to change. The Major rushed to put on his clothes. His hands fumbled with the buttons on his crisp white shirt as he tried to wrap his mind around what he'd just heard. *It's much bigger than I first imagined. Molotov must've had no problem making a case for others to sign on. I have to tell the American as soon as possible…*

Putting on his jacket, he stepped out of the men's changing room and towards the lobby where his car was waiting outside to take him to work. He replayed the impromptu exchange in his mind during the drive. *No, there wasn't anyone around paying attention to that drunk. You're overthinking things Pytor.*

Little had he noticed the lone figure discreetly hidden behind the towel cart.

2

The Second Day

It would be his last assignment. Carson Cooper contemplated that somber thought while looking out from his first-class window seat on the Boeing 737. Not too much longer now. Thirty minutes, he figured, before they landed at Sheremetyevo and it all began.

He pulled a cigarette from a small case he kept in the right pocket of his navy suit jacket. To anyone who asked, he'd given up the habit. Yet somehow, Cooper still found the ability to rationalize a puff just before going behind enemy lines. *If Cathy ever knew…well, she'd be at least happy to know that I've quit. Almost.*

What was it that the Deputy Director of Operations had said? He recalled the exact words spoken to him back in that corner office at Langley. "Now is a crucial moment for Moscow Station. Shroud, Torchlight, and all the rest of our assets there are extremely vital to staying one step ahead of the Soviets. You've seen the files. You, Director Casey, and I are the only ones who know their real names. Not even the President knows them. That's why we need a veteran, someone…"

"Old and grey?"

The Deputy Director looked across the room at what

appeared to be a relic from an era long ago. If you didn't know he'd been dead for over twenty years, you could've thought Cooper was a much older Clark Gable, right down to the mustache and large ears. His hair though, including the 'stache, was turning grey. Hard lines now marked the face that had served its country in clandestine operations for more than forty years. The Deputy privately questioned just how much the grizzled veteran had left in the tank.

"Yes. Let's just face the facts for a minute. We've stacked The Station with some incredible talent that's eager to hit the Russians in their own backyard. A lot of them, however, are wet behind the ears and on their first tour. We don't need you running about in the field. Those days are over Carson. Instead, we need someone to direct the troops and see that things get carried out properly."

Those days are over? Hmph! I'm in a lot better shape than you buddy. Maybe if you would get off your sorry…

"Attention passengers, we're now beginning our descent," said the captain over the intercom. "Expected arrival in Moscow will be approximately 8:45 a.m. local time. On behalf of British Airways, we would like to thank you for choosing us for your travel needs, and we hope you have a safe trip."

The old CIA veteran looked over his documents one more time. He would be entering the country on an official diplomatic visa. To anyone concerned, he was a member of the U.S. State Department with credentials signed by the President of the United States himself. *Yet they'll still have at least a half a dozen cars trailing us once we leave the airport.*

It was hard for him to accept. Despite a prestigious posting at a time when the Cold War seemed at its height, it felt more like being put out to pasture for the veteran case officer. All those unspoken operations in unnamed countries over the years had come down to this. Whether he liked it or not, he was giving up first-chair to become the conductor of his own small clandestine orchestra.

The plane finally touched down with the passengers exiting out onto the tarmac and into the terminal. Customs lay ahead. *Here we go.*

Reaching the front of the line, he approached the militia officer who examined each passport. The officer's eyes grew wide as he noted his special designation and made a gesture to a nearby colleague.

"Diplomat?"

"Yes," Carson said, clearing his throat. "There should be a car waiting to take me to the Embassy outside. First time here."

"Really? There are many great cultural sites you must see while here. I believe you'll be impressed. Welcome to the Soviet Union," he said in a matter of fact way as he stamped the passport and returned it to him.

Cooper could feel the piercing eyes already focused on him as he turned away from the officer. *Doveryay, no proveryay.* Trust but verify. *Yes, we may accept your passport, but we'll see if you really are just another American diplomat.*

Carson made a beeline to the loading and unloading area outside the gates and ticket counter. There he saw an African American man, about 5'9, medium build, and wearing a suit. He stood beside a black Cadillac. *Just like Langley ordered.* The two exchanged handshakes and made idle small talk as they put the bags into the trunk.

"You don't need to worry too much," the man said as they pulled away from the curb. "Car was checked for bugs early this morning and put under Marine guard in an isolated part of the garage."

"Good to know," he said while checking the rearview mirror.

"How was the flight?"

"Long. Do they always have seven following a mid-level State newbie?"

"You sure? I count six black Volga's."

"Red Warburg up ahead at the stop sign. You can just barely see the dirt left behind by the KGB's car wash."

"Impressive. Your eyes are better than mine. I'm Josh O'Neil, by the way. Everyone is looking forward to meeting you at the station. The Ambassador also asks you to come by Spaso House for lunch. He's pretty eager to meet you as well."

"Josh O'Neil? You're not the deputy COS are you?"

"What? You surprised? Oh, you think just because I'm black I can't do cloak and dagger," he said rather seriously.

"It did cross my mind," Cooper remarked with a smirk, but not flinching a bit.

O'Neil realized right away the new Chief of Station

wasn't going to be ruffled easily or pretend to ignore the obvious. "I'm just messing with you," he laughed. "Does make a good cover though. Surveillance seems to have bought into the idea that, because I stick out like a sore thumb, I'm the last person who'd try anything."

"Combine that thinking with the tricks brought to you by the Office of Technical Services, and you've got yourself one powerful cover," said Carson.

He may not have known who his Deputy would be, but he'd read O'Neil's file like all the rest of the case officers in Moscow and was genuinely impressed. Born to sharecroppers in Mississippi, he'd volunteered for the Marines rather than wait for the draft. Two tours later in Vietnam, O'Neil earned a silver star and moved on into intelligence. Once back stateside, he joined the CIA and showed an uncanny ability to succeed at whatever task, in the field or behind-the-desk analysis, he received. Carson knew right away that O'Neil was someone he could trust.

It was a forty-five minute drive to the Embassy. Passing through the northwest part of the Soviet capital, Carson looked out onto a bleak landscape full of Stalinist era block-style apartment buildings amidst overcast skies. The snow was on the ground. What else would there be in late winter?

Finally, they turned onto Bolshoy Devyatinsky. "Here we are," O'Neil observed. Carson noted the massive eleven-story Executive Office Building. It had been home for the U.S. diplomatic corps now for thirty years. With that said, however, it had seen more than its fair share of trouble. Besides the countless number of listening devices discovered over the years and harmful microwaves directed towards the building, it had caught on fire in the seventies, resulting in KGB officers disguised as firemen attempting to steal sensitive information. If not for the swift actions of the former Chief of Station blocking the firefighters' entrance into the CIA station's offices, it could've been even more devastating. Construction had started on a new chancery building adjacent to the compound five years earlier, though its completion date was way behind schedule thanks to 'reliable' Soviet labor.

O'Neil rolled down the window as they stopped alongside the guardhouse. A young Marine stepped forward and asked to see their identification before letting them through the gate.

"Right this way," the Deputy Chief of Station said with a smile as they pulled into his assigned spot. The two exited the vehicle and headed out of the parking garage and into the Executive Building. Once indoors, O'Neil led them onto an elevator. Neither saying a single word lest the KGB had gotten one of the Soviet nationals to plant a bug inside. Exiting on the ninth floor, they passed two marine guards who verified their credentials, before walking down a hall and taking a private back stairway to the seventh floor. There, they stopped at the fifth door on their left with a key code lock. O'Neil quickly punched in the code and both men stepped inside. Another door, this one a large titanium vault with a combination lock, lay just beyond. It stood open, unlocked earlier that morning when the first CIA officers arrived for work. The two passed through and continued down a short hallway before finally entering the small windowless room from which the Central Intelligence Agency ran their operations within the heart of the Soviet Union: Moscow Station.

"Here we are. Welcome to the Station! Everyone, I want to introduce our new Chief of Station, Carson Cooper."

About six people, mostly in their late twenties to mid-thirties, stood up from their desks and came over to welcome their new boss. Like O'Neil, he'd read up on each one, including even their spouses who regularly assisted them on various rendezvous with agents.

"Good to meet you sir," said a tall young man with mop of dirty blond hair wearing a navy turtleneck. "Name's James Shephard."

"I know," Cooper replied. *So this is the guy tasked with handling Torchlight.* The new COS sized up the young case-officer in charge of one of the most important spies to the U.S. "We've got a lot to discuss. Tell you what, I've a meeting right after this introduction over at Spaso. You have time to talk later this afternoon?"

"Should sir. I've got to report back to my desk duties with State on the third floor but I can get away for a bit."

"Sounds good. And just one more thing: call me Carson. If we're going to be working together, just this small group of us, no reason to not be on a first-name basis."

***

"You should have seen the party we threw the other night. Ray Charles played on the piano here in the

Chandelier Room". Carson stopped for a moment and tried to imagine The Genius performing *I Can't Stop Loving You* right there in the main hall of Spaso House. He'd always loved good jazz music.

"You should get David Brubeck here," Carson said to Ambassador Hartman. "What I wouldn't give to hear *Take Five* in person."

"Now that would be something. I have to credit Dona though. She's the one who puts all these fantastic evenings together. She loves to entertain."

The new Chief of Station and the U.S. Ambassador to the Union of Soviet Socialist Republics had just finished up an early lunch and were now touring the residence. Built seventy years prior by a textile industrialist before the Bolshevik Revolution, it had been the official residence of U.S. Ambassadors since the early days of Stalin.

The two stepped into the library. The room was marked by floor-to-ceiling windows on two sides with a small fireplace and a U-shaped arrangement of patterned fabric sofas on top of a large red rug. Hartman motioned for them to take a seat.

"I tell you though, it's been quiet in terms of diplomatic drama. We did have Vice President Bush here for Brezhnev's funeral last November, but otherwise nothing too crazy."

"Makes your job a whole lot easier, I guess," replied Cooper.

"It does. That's part of why I wanted to meet with you as soon as you arrived. I realize that as part of your job, you have to take a certain amount of risks to deliver the results our intelligence community requires. I'd like to ask, however, that you minimize that risk."

Cooper tilted his head with a confused expression. This was one of those times he didn't care about concealing his thoughts.

"Really?"

A tall man with distinct silver hair, Hartman sat up straight and looked Cooper directly in the eyes. "Everything may be tranquil momentarily, yet there's a lot at stake. We're dealing with a new General Secretary for the first time in years. You and the rest of the spies at the CIA have gathered up some useful intel on him. Still though, we're trying to learn who we're dealing with. Along with that, we've got a President who's using some of the staunchest rhetoric to describe this nation in recent memory."

"Nothing wrong with calling an evil empire an evil empire."

"I'm not commenting per se on his choice of words. What I am trying to say is that while both sides have attempted a state of détente, it could all be easily thrown out the window at the smallest mistake. My job is to smooth the wrinkles and keep the lines of communication open."

"I assure you Mr. Ambassador, we'll work to keep from rocking the boat. If we're performing our jobs correctly, no one should know what we're doing."

Hartman smiled at that. "Glad to hear it. I know it's only your first day, but is there anything you have for me? I'm sure you've been reviewing the situation here in your preparation for the position."

"Well sir, I want to look into it further, but in reviewing the security situation here, I think more steps could be taken to prevent intrusions. To be clear, this situation has existed for a long time before you or the previous Ambassador arrived in Moscow."

"Go on."

"For starters, we need to tighten access to sensitive areas in the Embassy. It's not a secret that the KGB handpicks every Soviet national that works here. They're here to get ahold of all the intel they can and then go use it against us."

"I see where you're coming from Carson. However, we also need to balance our responsibility with diplomacy."

"I'm sorry, but what does that have to do with diplomacy?"

"We need to show the Russian people that we're not afraid of them—that we trust them—if we're ever going to build towards a better relationship."

"With all due respect sir, we don't trust them. We are heavily concerned about their intentions. If you're going to build towards any sort of a 'better relationship,' then we need to keep our country in the stronger position by taking decisive action in the sphere of intelligence."

Hartman attempted a weak smile. "They told me you're known for not holding back."

If only you knew what I really think…

"I'm only offering you my honest assessment of

things as I've seen them through the lenses of an intelligence officer. You have to make the call how you see fit."

"Well, I need to be going. I've a meeting at the Embassy. You can ride with me if you'd like."

That would be the end of that discussion. Leaving the room, Carson was torn about how he felt towards the Ambassador. On the one hand, he liked him. Personally, at least. He seemed to care about putting forth his best efforts and highlighting the greatness of his country in the communist capital. On the other hand, however, he was leaving dangerous openings for the KGB to infiltrate and cause damage.

At least you know where things stand. Every officer will just have to work with the plain fact that nothing is ever fully secure outside the vault.

3

The Third Day

O'Neil saw the signal. Taking his regular morning jog, he began at the diplomatic compound and ran down the same streets each and every weekday. It had become predictable to the point that the KGB's surveillance had grown lax, often times leaving it to the militia men posted along the route to report their sightings of him. It was halfway through his run that the Deputy Chief of Station looked across the street at a particular apartment, up to the eighth floor, third and fourth windows from the right.

Tonight? What's so important that he needs to move up the meeting?

The shades on the third window, belonging to Major Pyotr Ivanovich, were halfway drawn up and open while the fourth's shades were closed in reverse. *Guess we'll see how the new sheriff in town handles it.*

An hour later, O'Neil reported what he saw to his boss at Moscow Station. The Chief of Station had yet to even have his first cup of coffee on the job when he learned of the signal.

"You see anything else?" Carson asked once he was finished.

"No sir. Like I said before, security around me is

light. If anyone gets near, I can spot them fast. It seems like the real deal."

Just then, James Shephard entered the Station to start the workday.

"Change of plans, James," said Cooper. "You're meeting in person with Torchlight tonight."

"What?"

"We just received word that he's signaled he wants to talk sooner than planned. He could have something important. He could also very well be compromised. You know the drill. Use your gut instinct on this one. If something doesn't seem right, abort the meeting and get out of there. Remember, you'll have Shroud with you as well. We don't need to put her at risk too."

"Understood."

"By the way, speaking of Torchlight, the care package for him arrived this morning."

Shephard looked to his right to see the Chief of Station get up from his desk.

"Did they get everything he asked for?" Shephard asked.

"Medicine for his wife. Pink Floyd, Led Zeppelin, and Whitesnake albums for his son. Poem collections by Joseph Brodsky, several of the latest issues of Time magazine. The only thing missing from the package is a cassette tape of Billy Joel."

"Any particular reason for it not being there?"

Cooper shrugged his shoulders. "They didn't give a

reason. Just plain forgot it seems."

Shephard walked over to a wall with a large map of the city taped to it. Various pins marked dead drops and rendezvous points. *How could a high ranking Soviet Union official like Torchlight be a member of the upper echelon of Soviet society, yet still have basic needs and wants only met west of the Berlin Wall?* Yes, the CIA did pay their agent well via a secret bank account, should he ever need to be extracted. The packages meant so much to him though, and for good reason. His wife's chronic asthma had greatly improved since she had begun taking American medicine, rather than what had been prescribed by Soviet doctors. Meanwhile, Torchlight had made a breakthrough in his quest to connect with his teenage son who, despite being the son of a KGB officer, had a particular curiosity for rock music.

Shephard turned his attention to several photos pinned to the side of the map. He'd taken these three weeks ago while scouting out a new location. He and his agent never had any sort of contact at the same place more than once. This time they would meet by the Moskva River of off *Kalininsky Prospekt.*

"I've also got two new Tropel T-50's for you to give him," Cooper said. "I know we talked about it last night, but remind him to be mindful of the lighting when snapping photos of documents. Langley wasn't able to make out some of the papers from the last batch of film. Most of it was still good, but, of course, they're wanting to gain as much intelligence as they can from him."

Shephard nodded. "Most valuable asset—that's what he is to this country. I only wonder how much longer his run can last."

"Hard to tell. He's lasted longer than Oleg Penkovsky ever did."

"Now," Cooper spoke, a bit louder to get everyone's attention in the Station. "Let's go over the plan for tonight. Carpenter and Brock should be back soon, and then we can go over some new surveillance hotspots the Russians have put in place. Doug, how's... Doug, are you listening?"

Doug Brown, a liaison from the Office of Technical Services, was sitting at a table, face down at work with a pair of headphones on. Another case officer walked over and pulled them off, catching him by surprise. Listening for a moment to the music coming from the headphones, she began to tap her foot. "Billy Joel. This a new album?" Lying on the table was a cassette of The Piano Man's new album, *An Innocent Man*, which she picked up and looked over.

"Does Torchlight have a Walkman?" she asked.

Shephard turned to Cooper with a smirk on his face. He then walked over and snatched Doug's Sony Walkman as well as the headphones.

"Hey! What gives?" protested Doug who had an irritated look on his face.

"He does now."

***

Boris Alexeev was clueless about his wife. He always thought it was his looks, class or maybe even his charm that had won the affection of the most beautiful woman to come from Kaliningrad. The hard facts, however, were that she neither married him for said attributes, nor did she come from Kaliningrad.

He awoke early that cold and snowy Monday morning to the familiar garish sound coming from the pipes within the walls. She was already up and showering. *Hopefully there will still be some warm water left.* He yawned and did his best to shake off the sleepy stupor. It wouldn't be too long until his car arrived to take him to the Kremlin.

Boris entered the steam-filled bathroom just as his wife was turning off the water. She stepped out from behind the shower curtain, dripping wet, and quickly grabbed a towel hanging nearby. Still enough time for Boris to take in an eyeful.

Tatiana's deep blue eyes met his, eliciting a somewhat dumbfounded expression on the young man's face. She gave a playful, flirtatious smile in return. "Good morning," she said while gripping the towel around her. "Did you sleep well last night?"

"I did. Especially after..." he started to say just as she leaned in and interrupted with a long, slow kiss.

"Mmm, me too. You better start getting ready. I'll have breakfast waiting when you're finished."

And to think I almost didn't go to that party for Veselovsky. I would've never met her!

Twenty minutes later, he was seated at the table, dressed for the day in one of his newer suits with a dark red tie, along with a hammer and sickle pin on his lapel. He alternated between sips of coffee and bites of toasted black bread while reading *Pravda*.

"Anything interesting?" she asked while starting to clear some of the dishes.

"*CSKA Moscow* won four to zero last night and Viacheslav Fetisov scored two goals. I'd like to take Nikita to the game next week if work doesn't get in the way."

"His coach told me when I picked him up from practice Monday that he's become the best right wing on the team. Maybe he'll make the national team one day."

The proud father beamed at the statement. "Maybe. Whatever he does, he'll be a success at it. The boy is hard-working and sharp."

"You said if work doesn't get in the way. Anything important?"

"Meetings, speeches to be reviewed, tasks to be administered. All the sorts of stuff a regular Politburo member's staff must handle."

"Sounds boring."

"Tatiana, I love you, but you've never had a mind for politics or party business. It's okay. In every other regard, you're splendid." At this, he rose from the table and prepared to head out the door.

She walked over to him and wrapped her arms around his waist. "Good, because if you said anything different, you'd be on your own for dinner from now on."

He kissed her softly on the lips. "I'd best be going. Where are the kids?"

"Sergei, Nikita, come say goodbye to your father."

Their two sons, ages six and eight, ran from the living area where they were watching TV and hugged him. He kissed them both on the cheek. For all the hardships and struggles of Russian society, Boris was like many others who still loved and valued their kids.

"Both of you behave yourselves and do what your mother says. I'll be home tonight and maybe we can watch some hockey before bed."

"Yeah!"

Tatiana peered out the kitchen window. "The car just pulled in front of the lobby."

"Okay, I'm off now. *Do svidaniya*!"

Once outside, his driver opened the backseat door of a GAZ Volga for him to hop in. It was only a few minutes' commute from his apartment to the Kremlin. The roads were crowded this morning, but not for the Volga. The exclusive median lane was made available to him due to his status as a senior personal staffer to Mikhail Gorbachev, the youngest full member of the Politburo. Boris looked out on the vast sea of cars belonging to the proletariat stuck in traffic. He thought about Tatiana. Taking the kids to school, shopping, lunch with her friends at the Leningradskaya Hotel—she had her routine like all Soviets and rarely if ever deviated from it. Did she enjoy it like he did his own?

If Boris could have followed Tatiana Alexeev closely that day, he'd have realized just how wrong he was. It came at the Leningradskaya. There amongst her friends, mostly wives of *nomenklatura* such as Boris.

"I mean it, I'd rather shop at GUM no matter the lines than go back to that marketplace in Kyiv ever again," remarked one woman in between mouthfuls of caviar.

"The only place Sacha says is worthwhile to buy anything outside of Moscow is Budapest. Though I hear some of it is black market," another replied.

Just then their waiter, a rather short man, middle-aged with a receding hairline, returned to the table. He had worked here at the Leningradskaya's restaurant for more than twenty years, providing exceptional service that made the place well-known both with Muscovites and tourists alike.

"May I take your plate for you, madam?" he said to Tatiana.

"Thank you…actually, no. I think I may have room for one more bite."

The waiter set the plate, which he'd barely picked up, back onto the table, smiled and continued to serve the rest of the dining party. Not a single person had seen the brush pass. A sleight of hand that would make a magician proud. While everyone who was paying attention saw only the near-empty plate, the waiter had in fact dropped a single scrap of paper from the napkin cloth into her lap. Tatiana casually placed it in her pocket before he turned to serve the rest.

She waited until later back at the apartment that afternoon to read what it said. Alone, she regularly checked the place for listening devices and cameras, always careful to make note of them rather than remove them and raise suspicion. The bathroom with just one bug above the cabinet next to the sink, and no windows, was the safest room.

Once decoded, the message read:

"Torchlight meeting at 19:00 tomorrow night. Be at safe house III before – Shepherd."

Tomorrow evening? Barely a heads up. Guess I can make it work though. Hopefully there'll be enough time before. With that, the Russian housewife tore the note to shreds, flushing the scraps down the toilet before starting work   on   the   family   laundry.

4

The Fourth Day

The unmarked van pulled out of the Embassy and onto the main street at half-past nine. James Shephard sat in the back, while the parts & supply officer drove and Cooper called shotgun. Under the guise of a maintenance crew, the van was often able to traverse the streets of Moscow with little to no surveillance. With a hidden wireless earpiece in the pocket of his overcoat, Shephard listened for any radio traffic between KGB officers running surveillance on them.

The case officer for Torchlight recalled his training from when he first joined the CIA: learning how to shake off anyone following him and beat surveillance at night on the streets of Baltimore. It was only after a twelve-hour run that began in a crowded shopping mall and ended with him meeting his 'contact' at Fort McHenry National Monument (and outwitting his instructor who was surveillance) did he finally graduate from The Farm. It felt so challenging then, Shephard reflected, yet now seemed like a cakewalk compared to roaming the streets of Moscow against America's greatest adversary.

Typically, the van made its runs throughout the day and into the evening as the parts and supply officer looked to gather whatever he needed for projects. His moves were often predictable. As a result, he encountered less surveillance than others at Moscow Station.

Not a word was spoken as they drove through the streets. The noise Shephard was hearing over the scanner was light. There hadn't yet been any radio chatter at all about their vehicle. Still, they would spend an hour or two driving around, hoping to sniff any surveillance out and lose it fast.

Up front, Cooper did his best not to pull at the disguise he wore, consisting of an elaborate mask and a vinyl bald cap. Special thanks was in order to the Office of Technical Services and the help of a Hollywood make-up artist working as a contractor. The Chief of Station's appearance gave no hint of the distinct mustache he bore but was instead marked with noticeable reddish eye brows. He'd reviewed every detail of the meeting thoroughly, leaving nothing to chance. *No way are we going to stumble out of the gate. Not in the first week here.*

"The next turn. That should work," whispered Shephard from behind to the parts officer as they sat at a light. They'd managed by now to identify two cars trailing from behind. The parts officer saw the noticeable triangle patch of dirt on the grills of both vehicles, a clear sign they had been through the KGB car wash. Shephard strongly desired to exit the vehicle when he could be in the black and outside of surveillance, but it wouldn't be easy. He would have to take advantage of a small, momentary blind spot when they could speed up and round a corner, allowing him to jump out of the van and blend into the streets as an evening pedestrian.

The light turned green, and they were moving again. He would have ten seconds, maybe, to make the jump out of the car and disappear. They were now approaching the turn at the corner.

Cooper checked the rearview mirror. "Get ready".

The van began slowing for Shephard. The corner where he would be exiting appeared poorly lit. No one stood about. He began sliding open the side door as they made the turn. Quickly, the young CIA officer jumped out in a side rolling motion. It wasn't the first time he'd jumped out of a moving vehicle. Still, his bones ached as his body hit the pavement. A rush of adrenaline dulled the pain and kept him focused on the mission.

He swiftly got up and began walking forward at a brisk pace as the van sped away. Moments later the two KGB cars rounded the corner, unaware of the lone man in the shadows walking along the sidewalk, as they continued following the decoy.

Up ahead was a small dry cleaners. Located along a sleepy sidewalk, its storefront signage was marked in fading Cyrillic letters painted in a drab grey. No passerby ever assumed what its true purpose was. Stepping inside, Shephard approached the counter where a man sat distracted, watching a hockey match on a small television.

"Yes?"

"I'm here to pick up the blue cashmere sweater I dropped off yesterday."

"There seems to be a mark or stain of some kind. Come, let me show you."

Shephard was led towards the back, past a myriad of hanging clothes to the door of an isolated room. He nodded to the man who returned to his TV.

Entering the windowless room, only one person was waiting for him: a woman, young and attractive, who appeared nearly finished putting on a disguise. Shephard's face brightened up when he saw her.

"Hey. You ready for tonight?"

"Yep, almost. Just this wig and glasses and I should be ready."

He came over and wrapped his arms around her from behind. "Wait, one second. I need a moment to take in the real you before you finish putting on that ensemble."

Tatiana Alexeev shook her head as she pulled away. "You're impossible." She gave him a quick peck on the cheek before putting the short curly-haired wig on and getting it in place. "How do I look?"

"Not like the wife of someone working in the Kremlin," he chuckled.

She was disguised as a working-class member, right down to the motor oil stain on her left shoe. For good measure, she'd be walking a dog belonging to the owner of the cleaners.

"Need to let you that there's been a change of plans. Torchlight wants a meeting, in-person."

"What? He's a KGB Major! He ought to have more sense than that," she exclaimed in a lowered voice.

"It's what he wants," he said with a shrug. "We'll just have to be extra vigilant. If you see anything tonight, anything that looks like surveillance, I need to know ASAP."

"Better be good whatever he's got," she muttered as she looked in the mirror one more time.

"Hasn't let us down yet."

Shephard began to change into his own disguise for the evening. He began by casually turning his black patterned jacket inside out, revealing a dark chestnut color. Next, he applied side burns to each side of his head that matched his dirty blond hair. Then, to give the appearance of one much older than his twenty-nine years, he applied make-up under his eyes to give the impression of puffiness, as well as a prosthetic double chin.

"How do I look?" he asked, placing his hands on his hips and cocking his head slightly in a goofy pose.

"Like Peter Sellers, if he got lost in Russia looking for the Pink Panther."

"Tough crowd. Well, it should still do the trick."

Like so many other men, Shephard found himself mesmerized by Tatiana. He was instantly attracted from the moment they first met and not just for her looks. The strength she showed living a double life while staying seemingly cool and calm was what he most admired. He never knew her real name. Only the Director of the CIA, the Assistant Director of Operations, and the new COS knew her actual identity. Instead, he would call her 'blue eyes'.

Any ideas the spy had of something more than a working relationship were in vain, however. Tatiana was a realist to the core. In a world of secrets and lies, she knew romance was out of the question. Leave that to Hollywood. She had a job to do for her country—a job she took seriously and handled with extreme precision.

"We better get going," she said. "The car is the back alley."

Shephard walked alongside the Moskva River at a leisurely pace while waiting for Torchlight. There were still quite a few pedestrians taking an evening stroll and heading home after a long workday. The case officer kept his eyes open for his agent while Tatiana watched for any surveillance as she walked her Siberian husky.

Twenty yards or so ahead of him, he noticed an older gentleman strolling along with a noticeable white stain on the right elbow of his dark overcoat. Everything was still on track. Shephard quickened his pace. Getting closer, he scanned the surrounding area for anyone that might be watching. No more than a step behind his agent, he knew he was in the black.

The seasoned CIA officer slowed for a second before deciding his course of action. Taking a deep breath, he moved alongside Torchlight. "Park bench to the right," he uttered in Russian as he continued past him.

Torchlight said not a word, but followed. Shephard led the way toward a lone park bench off to the side of the sidewalk and sat down first.

Major Pyotr Ivanovich took a seat opposite his much younger handler and continued to avoid eye contact. Neither said a word as the Major removed a cigarette from a pack he had inside the left pocket of his overcoat and lit it. Slowly he brought it to his lips and inhaled before exhaling a cloud of white smoke that seemed to give off an aura of mystery.

"You must know that I've only requested to speak face-to-face to discuss a serious matter," the Major said slowly.

"Go on," Shephard replied as he looked down into the open book he held.

"There is a man who serves as a full voting member on the Politburo. He is younger than his colleagues and has shown signs of being open to certain ideas of reform. The General Secretary holds him in high regard. His rise to power is seen as a threat to many of the old guard. It's for this reason that they've made plans to kill him soon."

"Okay. Why not just put all this in a message and leave it in the dead drop?" *Instead of putting all of us at risk like this*, thought a frustrated Shephard. "I don't think I have to tell a KGB officer with more than thirty years of experience that meeting like this at the last second is dangerous."

"To show you the fear in my eyes if they should succeed. Look at me," Ivanovich said facing his case officer. Shephard turned his head and saw the look of a man sincerely troubled and afraid.

"What exactly do you expect my country to do about it?"

"To stop it. At all costs. The details can be found inside this," Ivanovich answered as he subtly pulled out the cigarette carton and placed it beside him on the bench. "I must go."

With that, Torchlight abruptly continued on his evening stroll. Shephard reached for the carton and put it inside his jacket. Time to get back to the Embassy right away. The van would be waiting for him just a few blocks from here.

Across the park, three men out of view had just finished capturing photographs of the encounter. Earlier that afternoon the officers of the 2nd Directorate had been ordered to run full surveillance on their superior. Now they had the evidence they needed. The most senior of the three picked up his radio receiver. "Move in on both targets." Immediately, a dozen plainclothes officers rushed towards their traitorous colleague and his CIA friend.

5

Tatiana's ear rang with a loud squealing sound made by the nearby KGB radio transmission. Pulling the earpiece away, she saw several men moving in about 150 yards to Shephard's right. She quickly gave two clicks on the radio in her pocket and hoped he heard the signal.

Shephard's entire body tensed up as he realized what was happening. Instinct and training suddenly collided. He began moving at a pace just short of a jog. Two groups of KGB men were now visibly approaching from two directions. Up ahead on the pathway was a crowd of people. If he could just get lost among them for a moment…

Tatiana, meanwhile, stayed calm. She knew they weren't after her. The deep-cover spy was invisible to them.

Suddenly, she spotted James moving in her direction. His eyes locked onto hers for just a moment as he neared the cluster of pedestrians. They said all she needed to know.

He wants to make a brush pass. That'll mean getting closer and mixing in with the throng up ahead.

They were coming nearer now. So was the 2nd Directorate. Shephard held tight to the cigarette carton in his pocket as he moved ahead into the flow of people. Whatever happened, he had to get the package away from here and back to the Station.

He was now approaching on Tatiana's left with the dog walking in front of her. In the midst of the crowd of pedestrians, there was little chance the KGB could see the brush pass that was about to happen. Holding her left hand open at her side, she took hold of the carton as Shephard passed. Yet he didn't let go.

The rush of adrenaline and anxiety had left his hand uncontrollably clinched. The carton ripped in two. Tightly folded papers fell to the ground.

Stop? Not a chance. Tatiana instantly chose to keep moving forward. Shephard looked back disgustedly to see the contents lying on the ground. No one passing by seemed to be paying any notice to either what had happened or the torn papers resting on the pavement. Momentarily he thought about walking back and picking them up before realizing it would be in vain.

The move into the crowd had bought him only a few extra seconds of respite. Another KGB officer with the detail was watching the street when Shephard hurried towards the nearest metro station. He saw the young CIA officer and quickly yelled at two militiamen nearby to arrest him. They chased after him as he began to run down the stairs, over the turnstiles, and to the platform. His only hope was to lose them once more in a crowd.

Quickly he attempted to turn his coat outside in as he mixed into the waiting group of people. He could see the next train coming through the tunnel and nearing the station just now.

"Stop him! He's an enemy of the *Rodina*!"

They were speeding down to the platform now—
at least eight of them altogether. The train abruptly
came to a complete stop. Passenger doors opened as
Shephard lurched forward, eagerly pushing past the
proletariat who were just beginning to realize the
situation. None wished to be anywhere near him, lest
they be accused of acting as an accomplice.

Aboard, he headed to the back of the passenger
car on the farthest end. There in that car about a
dozen people sat in their seats exhausted, ready to go
home at the end of a long day. A couple passengers
watched him with an air of concern. He found a spot
across from one of them and tried to get his heavy
breathing under control. *Were they still following?*

The metro train's side doors slammed shut as they
began to move. *Just stay seated. They can't see you.* The
next seven minutes felt like the longest seven of
Shephard's life. In all his time at Moscow Station, he
noted that this was the closest he'd come to being
arrested. *If you can just get back inside the Embassy, you'll be
safe. Then maybe we can unpack this story from Torchlight.
Speaking of, did he escape?*

Finally, the train slowed and entered the next
station. He stepped off with the rest of the passengers
leaving and walked casually toward the stairway to
return back up to the street. Had he lost them, he
wondered? Scanning the platform with his eyes, he
saw no obvious members of the KGB.

James moved up the stairs now, his heart still
beating fast. If he were to make it out of this alive, he
would need to keep on the move until morning. Only

then could he return to the Embassy. Simply going back to his apartment was not an option. The KGB no doubt had informants both right outside of and at the diplomatic compound where nearly everyone from State lived.

"Excuse me, comrade." He heard those words in English just as a firm hand took hold of his right shoulder. Shephard reached to pull the hand away before another arm yanked his left arm back.

"I suggest you do not resist. You're under arrest."

Tatiana stepped into the shadowy alley behind the cleaners, still out of breath. She'd been on the move for the last two hours, making double-sure no one was following. There was no telling what had happened to James, though she feared the worst. *Torchlight had to have already been under surveillance.*

She closed her eyes and let out a deep sigh. She felt the torn carton in her inner coat pocket and remembered what James had given her. *Something Torchlight must've passed to him.* This wasn't the place to pull it out and examine the contents. She needed to get home soon, but first, she had to change back into the wife of a Kremlin official.

Back inside the windowless room, Tatiana carefully removed the brown wig first, followed by the pair of glasses. She let down her hair, then reached for a bottle of vodka sitting on a side table and poured herself a shot. She threw the shot glass back in hopes of calming her nerves.

The ripped carton was still in her coat pocket

when Tatiana pulled it out. Only one folded piece of paper remained. On it was but a list of names, written in the style of a shaky hand. Her eyes read over them slowly. *General Vladimir Sorokin. Minister Misha Burdin. Colonel Damir Petrov.* The list went on from the highest-ranked in the Soviet bureaucracy to those of less stature and more obscure. Halfway through reading, she paused. *What exactly do all these men have in common?* There was nothing else written on the back to give a clue. Tatiana continued reading. She was so focused on her frustration at the lack of clarity that she nearly missed the name near the bottom.

Boris Aleexev. Her heart nearly stopped. Her Boris?

It was nearly eleven as Tatiana neared the apartment. Just around the corner, across the street, and she'd soon be home. Up ahead on the corner stood a mailbox. As she neared it, she reapplied her lipstick once more and, without stopping her walk, drew a red streak across the side of a rusted teal colored mailbox.

***

Save for a single overhead light, a tired James Shephard found the interrogation room to be both a dark and pessimistic place. Then again, that description fit just about anywhere inside this part of the Lubyanka Building. It was often said by many that this was the tallest building in Moscow, for one could see Siberia from its basement. Under standard procedure, however, Shephard was unlikely to be heading to the cold eastern frontier of the Soviet Union. Instead, just as he was taught to should the situation arise, he would continue to plead his case that he was but an American diplomat who'd done nothing wrong. The KGB would say otherwise, followed by the American Ambassador receiving a call to pick him up. He would be turned over to the Ambassador, quickly declared persona-non-grata, and be sent home for good. Once home, Langley would want a thorough de-briefing.

He'd been waiting for only a few minutes in between two guards when a rather short middle-aged man, somewhat balding, was allowed into the room. He said not a word until he took a seat at the opposite end of a cheap wooden table where Shephard sat.

"Doing more than just diplomatic work tonight, Mr. Shephard?" he said in English.

"Pardon me, sir, but I don't get what you're insinuating. I'm an American citizen, working as a diplomat within the U.S. State Department at the Embassy. I was returning home from an evening stroll when I was arrested with no good cause."

"You were found with a hidden radio and earpiece as well as some rather peculiar items in your possession. Forgive me if I beg to differ."

"Again, I'm an American diplomat and demand to speak with my Ambassador."

The small man shook his head as a wry smile marked his face. "We shall see. But first I want to get to…"

The door swung open again as another man entered. A high-ranking KGB officer by the look of his uniform, he had an air of authority about him.

"Comrade Boriski, you can go. I shall handle this matter." He nodded to the guards standing on each end of the diplomat. "You will leave as well."

There was silence in the room for several moments once everyone had left. Shepherd and the man stared at each until finally, the Russian spoke. "My name is General Dmitri Medved. It is too bad that you had to make contact with your agent tonight. Actually, it is too bad that you ever came to our country."

"I'm an American diplomat who demands to speak with my…"

"Enough. You will not be speaking with anyone, Mr. Shephard. You will not be leaving here. Maybe, only maybe, will you live to see another day, if you will tell me what I want to know."

"I know nothing."

"Oh, you can continue pretending you're innocent with that confused look on your face. But we both know what I'm talking about. If the shoe was on the other foot and a rising politician in your country championed ideas that you believed undermined your government's very existence, would you not do everything in your power to stop that?"

Shephard said not a word.

"Perhaps" remarked the General. "But then again, perhaps not. Tell me, where has your friend Major Ivanovich gone to? You both left so suddenly."

Shephard continued to remain stone-faced silent.

Realizing he wasn't going to get anywhere, the Russian went to the door and spoke a few words to the man outside. When the door closed and he returned to the table again, he carried a tray with two meals and a bottle of vodka.

"Enough of this talk. I haven't eaten since morning and am starving. You shall join me." He poured Shephard a shot and handed it to him.

Shephard took the shot glass. He did his best to steady his hands, lest they tremble and betray his fear and anxiety at what he knew was soon to come. *So this is how it ends.* His mortality wasn't something he dwelled upon a lot. Now his mind was racing with thoughts on how he'd lived his life. The good, the bad, and how he wished he could've done some things over again differently.

As he felt the warmth of the vodka go down his throat, he thought of Shroud. He didn't doubt that she had gotten away. But the torn carton?

"Now, for the main course. Have you ever tried *pelmeni*? Some like to use beef for filling. Me, though, I prefer lamb. Much better taste."

They ate for a couple of minutes in silence. The General scarfed his down fast. Shephard ate slowly. The taste wasn't bad, at least not for what may be a final meal. If only for a moment, his thoughts became focused upon the plate before him.

General Medved poured several more drinks for him and his prisoner. He rambled on everything from spycraft to women to even pure bred horses until finally asking Shephard if he'd like some brandy instead. The now unwound American nodded and said yes.

"I shall step outside and see if we can't get some. One moment."

As he walked behind him and headed towards the door, Shephard's thoughts returned to Tatiana once more. Of everyone he'd come to know and work with, she had been the only one in this barren, cold dystopia that he'd cared about. Now he would never see her.

The General stood several paces behind the spy. He undid the cover from his holster and slowly removed his pistol.

Shephard's last act was a silent prayer. Never really a churchgoer, he found himself, like so many others in their final moments, humbled before his Maker. He prayed that God would take care of his mother back in Boise. He prayed for forgiveness for all the times he'd taken the easy path instead of the right one. And before the shot rang throughout that lonely basement room, he prayed they would somehow uncover the truth at Moscow Station.

6

The Fifth Day

The mood was downcast at Moscow Station that early morning. A mission compromised. A case officer and an agent missing. Cooper sat at his desk, preparing a report to send back to Langley. *What did we miss? Surveillance? An orchestrated trap? Missed signals?*

He'd waited all night for Shephard to return. The Station was completely in the dark as to what happened. All anyone could assume was that the meeting had gone wrong and arrests had likely been made.

But if arrests were made, why hasn't the Embassy Duty Officer received a call from the Foreign Ministry that they're holding one of our guys? Something is more than just wrong.

He desperately needed more intel before he reported back. Without it, he feared Langley would scrutinize every action from his last few days in charge and look for whatever excuse to pin it on his age.

Suddenly the vaulted security door swung open as Deputy Chief O'Neil entered the room. "Well, Shroud's alive at least!"

The old veteran breathed a sigh of relief. "The okay signal?" he asked.

"Yep. It appears she wants to meet. No trace of Shephard though, I'm afraid," replied O'Neil.

"Signal Shroud to meet at safe house III two days from now if they can."

"Who do you want to send?"

"No one. I'm going."

***

It was a day off for everyone in the Aleexev household. Boris slept in that morning while the children read the comics. Later that afternoon, Nikita had a hockey game to play. Tatiana, meanwhile, hadn't deviated from her routine one bit. She was preparing lunch when Boris came into the kitchen.

"Sleep well?"

"*Da.* How was dinner with your cousin?" He said as he noticed the bag of potato chips sitting on the counter and began snacking.

"Really nice. Thank you for being so understanding. It's been years since I last saw her."

"Family is important, no matter how long in between visits." He kissed her softly and then pressed his forehead to hers and stared into her eyes longingly. "Think you could make some snacks for the game?"

***

The last twelve hours had been anything but a cakewalk for Pyotr Ivanovich. Having seen his colleagues move in to arrest his handler, the Major hurried through the crowds using every trick in the books. He knew better than to return home. Instead, he was now taking refuge in an old friend's apartment. It'd been some time since they last spoke, but his friend would be nowhere near the top of the list of people the KGB would pay a visit.

"How are you feeling this morning?" Dima Turgenev asked as he walked into the small living area.

"A little bit better" replied Ivanovich. "Thank you for allowing me to stay here on your couch like this. What with Elina upset…"

"You're fine. What are friends for? You looked terrible when you knocked last night. It must have been some fight you had with your wife?"

"We don't usually have problems like that. I'll go and patch things up today. It will all be better."

Dima smiled. He may be a bachelor but at least he didn't have to deal with any domestic disputes like his friend the Major. "Good to hear. I'm going to fix some eggs for breakfast. Want any?"

"Please. Thank you Dima. You're as true a friend as there ever was."

His host went into the kitchen as he pondered his next move. He couldn't stay here for two nights in a row. Too risky. He would have to keep on the move.

But what about your wife and son? What's going to happen to them? You couldn't put it past the KGB to try and arrest them. No doubt they've already been questioned. The apartment most likely has been ransacked in their investigation. Somebody knew what was up. But who?

That wasn't the only question Pyotr was trying to answer. He had no way of knowing if the intel he passed to Shephard had successfully made it back to those who could intervene and attempt to stop this plot. *But how do you find that out when you're on the run?*

***

The safe house was a simple two-bedroom apartment at the very end of a hallway on the sixth floor of a building five miles away from the Embassy. Using a bit of tradecraft known as an identity transfer, Carson disguised himself to look exactly like a thirty-something-year-old State employee who worked at the Embassy. He even drove the man's car to the meeting. Meanwhile the employee, who'd long ago been deemed a highly unlikely intelligence threat by the KGB, was required to stay sitting dead quiet in a secure room until the Station Chief returned.

Nearing the door, Cooper took the key out from his pocket. He recalled reading the file on Shroud back at Langley. So much about her was a closely guarded secret. What he did know though, was that this CIA officer under non-official cover (NOC) had been through a lot—both before and after joining The Agency.

In the aftermath of Shephard's arrest, he feared the possibility that the KGB had faked the okay signal Shroud had given, waiting inside now to arrest whoever should enter first. He tried his best to shake the thought away as he unlocked the door.

Walking in, Cooper noted a long hallway stretching towards a small kitchen and a living room. He removed both his hat and jacket and placed it on the coat rack in the hall. There was already another coat there—one belonging to a woman.

He could hear footsteps now coming from the kitchen. Now walking out and into the darkened living room with shades pulled down. He couldn't see the face, only a silhouette from the light coming out of the kitchen. He reached over to turn on a lamp.

"You don't know how relieved I am to see you."

Shroud smiled. "That makes two of us. Good to finally meet you, sir."

"The name's Carson," he said as they shook hands. We've got a lot to discuss."

She looked him over for a moment, assessing just how old this guy was, as he began removing parts of his disguise. She hadn't met the last COS but figured he'd been at least twenty years younger than this guy.

"I went ahead and made some coffee in the kitchen. Can I get you some?"

"Appreciate it," he said, taking a seat while she went to go get him a cup.

"Cream and sugar?" she asked as she made her way to the kitchen.

"Always like mine black, thanks."

She came back with two mugs filled. "Good. Was always taught black was the only way to drink it."

"So. What all happened that night?"

Tatiana spent the next fifteen minutes going over everything that transpired that evening, including the torn carton and its remaining contents. She then handed him an envelope with the mysterious list of names.

"James say anything when he made the brush pass?"

"Not a word. I've read the list. Vast majority are on the Central Committee. Several are high-ranking KGB. Four are Politburo members. "

Carson pulled out a pair of glasses and read it over.

"Guess you already know your Russian husband is on here. Any guesses as to why that is?"

"Not a clue. Boris is well connected though, what with working for Gorbachev."

He paused for a moment, trying to decide how to convey what he had to say next. He knew it wouldn't be easy to hear.

"The Ambassador received word from the Foreign Ministry today about James," the COS said carefully. "Officially he was "found" dead in an alley by the Militia with a gunshot wound to the skull."

Her mouth fell open in total disbelief as he continued. "The KGB doesn't kill our officers working behind the shield of the State Department. Until now. James learned something nobody was supposed to find out about. We need to know what that is."

"Do they even realize they've broken literally the most important unwritten rule?" she said finally. "I...I can't believe..."

"I know. That's why it's imperative we now operate with that understanding. Be smart. Don't take any unnecessary risks."

She nodded in agreement. "So, what's next?"

"I'd be spitballing if I gave you an answer now. Once I get back, I'll send Langley what you gave me and await orders. Until then, you'll be directly reporting to me."

"Next meeting?"

"For now, we play it safe and use this," Carson said as he set two handheld devices on the table. The latest in wireless communication thanks to the technical gurus in the Office of Technical Services.

"What is it?"

"They call it a DISCUS. You might not have used any of the earlier models," he said as he handed one of them to her. "With this gadget, you can type an encrypted message and send it to me with the push of a button. Much more secure and a heck of a lot faster to communicate with."

Tatiana looked the device over. She had seen some early Short-Range Agent Communications devices years before when she first began training at The Farm. She also remembered the limited range those once had. "How close do I have to be?"

"If you were in your apartment near the Kremlin, you could send a message and have it be received while I'm sitting at my station desk."

"Not bad," she said while tilting her head to the side. Turning on the device, she began to type. Once finished, she hit send.

"Well, I imagine you would after ten years," he

laughed aloud as he read the instant message: 'Double-patty hamburger with barbecue sauce, fries, milkshake, and a Coke'. "Do you ever miss it? I mean, being back in the U.S. and not always looking over your shoulder?"

She brushed her hair back from her eyes and looked straight at her boss. "For ten years, this has been my life. After a while you get used to being alert, always ready, playing the part. Sometimes, I almost forget my real name."

"Audrey Davis."

"First time in a while I've heard that one. Yeah, sometimes I dream about what it would be like back stateside. I haven't forgotten why I do this. However..."

"You think it would be strange not to be playing the part?" he said. "I've heard of it before, especially for someone who's been at this as long as you have."

"I guess that's one way to put it. To play the part, you have to live it, to become it," she said with the fleeting sign of a grimaced expression.

Carson nodded. There was only so much he could say, yet so much he was thinking. Though she kept her cards close, he knew living a double life took a toll. The idea of extraction had been brought up once or twice by the Deputy Director before heading to the Soviet Union. Yet Carson felt he couldn't offer it, not with everything that had just happened. They needed someone with high-ranking connections, especially at a time like this.

Two hours later, the Chief of Station was back at

the Embassy. Walking down the hall, he made his way to the door of Chris Murray, the civilian NSA employee assigned to the Embassy. Moments after knocking, a short and wiry man in his mid-forties with a glass eye opened to see who it was.

"I've got a message for you."

"Okay. Any particulars?" Murray asked.

"Need this to be on a one-time pad. Top-secret."

"I hear ya loud and clear." Murray took the single folded sheet of paper with the written message to be transmitted for the top brass on the seventh floor's eyes only. He looked up at the COS.

"Long day?"

"Long week," Cooper said while rubbing his eyes. *Not even two weeks and you're already exhausted. An officer dead. An agent missing. It's got to look up from here.*

***

More than a thousand kilometers away as the Chief of Station prepared to call it a day, a local meeting of Polish Solidarity supporters in Warsaw was coming to a close inside a cellar. All who attended came from working class backgrounds. Each was united in his resolve for freedom and achieving it through non-violent means. All except one man.

"Thank you for coming Jozef. Will we see you at the next meeting?"

"I will be there, for sure" said Jozef Woźniak. Twenty-six years old and a machinist in an auto factory nearby, he had taken a keen interest in the new Polish Solidarity movement. When some of his co-workers mentioned three months ago attending a meeting, he eagerly asked if he might come along. Since then, he'd been a vocal attendee, speaking out earnestly in opposition to the Soviet occupation.

Woźniak stepped outside the cellar that led onto a cobbled street. He pulled a cigarette from a pack inside the left pocket of his jacket. As he lit it, he saw the full moon illuminating a clear night sky. Home was only a ten-minute stroll two blocks away.

"Excuse me," a man's voice called from behind as he walked back to his apartment. He continued onward, ignoring whoever it was, and quickened his pace.

A tap came on his shoulder. "Excuse me, sir. One moment please. I don't mean to bother you, but would you have a light?"

"Sure," he said while cautiously reaching in his jacket for his lighter.

"You think I was with the SB or something? Ah, thank you."

Woźniak returned the lighter to his jacket. "No. Just can't be sure of anyone these days."

"True. But what we can be sure of is a promising future, comrade."

Woźniak relaxed just a bit at this. "You're new. What happened to Gregory?"

"He's been reassigned to another part of the country. I'll skip with the introductions because this will be the only time we speak."

The man stopped to take a long drag from his own

cigarette.

"You were saying?"

"You've been activated," said the KGB officer. "It is   time."

7

The Sixth Day

Director of Soviet Operations Connor O'Leary had only glanced at the decrypted message five minutes earlier when he was summoned to the seventh floor of the Central Intelligence Agency's headquarters in Langley, Virginia.

He straightened his tie one more time. It was 5:30 a.m. He'd been at his desk all night and would give just about anything for a shower and six hours of sleep. The Torchlight incident, as the select few with the appropriate security clearance were calling it, was consuming every waking moment of his time. Still, it was the exact stuff that kept him going.

Deemed a 4-F and unable to see action in Vietnam, O'Leary had finished college and taken an entry-level analyst job fifteen years ago. He quickly excelled at pouring over countless pieces of intelligence in order to provide insightful analysis for the decision makers. That in turn had led to a series of promotions. Now he was tasked with unraveling the mystery Moscow Station had found itself in.

"The Deputy Director will see you now," said the secretary in the lobby.

O'Leary went inside, all the while rehearsing exactly what he would say to his boss.

Deputy Director of Operations David Palmer stood pouring himself a cup of coffee, his third so far that morning, from a maroon Texas A&M mug.

"Connor. Don't tell me you haven't gone home yet? You look beat."

"Afraid not sir. Been busy what with the murder of the case officer and whatever's become of Torchlight."

"I know. This new message from Cooper at the Station there only creates more d--ned questions," replied the Deputy Director.

David Palmer motioned for him to take a seat as he made his way over to a couch beneath a wall covered with framed photos. It had been a long and winding career for this clandestine relic. Straight out of the Corps of Cadets at A&M, Palmer had been an officer in Wild Bill Donovan's military intelligence division, the OSS, during the WWII. Afterward, he served in Army intelligence for a spell before joining the CIA in its infancy. He'd seen both the highs and the lows. Now, with a President in office who was serious about the threat of communism and unafraid to call the Soviets for what they were—an "evil empire"—the CIA had undergone a rebirth and was taking the offensive.

"So, what do you think Connor?"

"Sir, the information that we obtained is simply a list of names, albeit a list of some of the most prominent members of the Kremlin hierarchy. I don't mean to sound conspiratorial, but we can't rule out that certain elements of the KGB are covering up something. You don't break normal diplomatic protocol and kill an official member of the U.S. State Department without a justifiable cause."

"Reasonable theory," remarked Palmer. I don't like it one bit though. Especially when one of our own is dead because of it. Have a message sent back to Cooper. Tell him to do everything he can to find out what happened to Torchlight. He may already be dead, but if he isn't, he could be the key to solving this.

"For all we know, this could be anything from a rather embarrassing secret involving a bunch of power players to a full-on coup. I have a meeting with the Director in two hours, followed by another with the National Security Council Advisor. We need answers Connor. Get with the analysts and see if there are any important connections to the names on that list have. The President is furious and is eager to take action."

"I'll get on it right away, sir." The Soviet Operations Director started to turn to leave when Palmer added one last thing.

"And Conner. It might be nothing, but check in on that sleeper cell."

***

Carson sat at his desk while reading the directive. As he did so, he tossed a baseball straight into the air he'd once caught while seated along the third-base line at an Orioles game. It was a tall order. *Like finding a needle in a haystack. Can't exactly place an ad in Pravda and wait to hear back.*

There were still some lower-level assets in the KGB. Maybe they'd know if he'd been picked up. He could also have either one of his officers or an agent keep an eye on his apartment. Sooner or later, he just might come back or try to send a message.

One more idea came to mind. Carson took a key and unlocked a drawer in his desk. Pulling out the DISCUS, he thought through what he was going to message Shroud. Finally, he started typing.

"Brass want answers. Need to know what happened to the agent that night. Keep eyes/ears open regarding names on the list, especially Boris. Let me know ASAP if you have anything."

He pressed send and set the device down. Three minutes later, he got a reply.

"Understood. Boris and I are attending a Foreign Ministry reception this Thursday at the Bolshoi Theatre. Most of those names and their wives will be there."

That would work. Between what he'd read about Shroud and actually meeting her, there was little doubt in his mind that she would uncover some piece of valuable intel. The Deputy Director had made it clear, though: time was of the essence. That particular factor bothered him the most.

***

It was ribeye steaks on the menu for lunch at the Embassy commissary. Brought in special from Helsinki the day before, everyone eagerly waited for 11:15 to roll around. Chris Murray was no exception. Hastily, he got up from his desk in the small communications room and headed out the door.

Getting on the elevator, he passed Zinoviy, one of the janitors who regularly mopped the hallways on that particular floor.

No one ever seemed to notice janitors, who were all Soviet nationals, including Zinoviy. Now with lunch calling, the floor was nearly deserted but for this lone Russian.

Quickly, he glanced around before retrieving a duplicate key from his pocket. Unlocking the NSA employee's office door, Zinoviy pushed his cleaning equipment inside and shut the door behind him. He didn't have much time. There were no guarantees someone wouldn't get off the elevator at any moment and return to their office.

He immediately saw the small safe against the wall. If only the Embassy could've known their janitor was a professional safe-cracker, offered a deal by the KGB to avoid prison. This job, compared to his many previous heists, would be cinch.

Ten minutes later, the heavy steel door was open. Zinoviy wiped his brow and let out a sigh of relief. Still enough time before the Marine guard made their rounds throughout the floor in another five minutes. He pulled out a miniature camera similar to the CIA's Tropels and reached for the top folder. Communications, codes, secret cables—there was no way of being able to read and discern what was of high value. He instead snapped away until the camera ran out of film and then reached into his pocket for another.

"I'll see you guys down there. This will only take a few minutes."

He'd lost track of time! Putting the folder back, Zinoviy slammed the safe shut and turned off his flashlight.

A diagonal sliver of light came through the cracked door as the guard came up the hall, checking each door that typically remained locked at this time. The janitor carefully shut the office door and locked it back, holding his breath as the Marine neared.

The advancing footsteps stopped. The doorknob jiggled loudly, causing Zinoviy to jump and nearly knock over a chair. He reached to steady it. The guard however wasn't moving on. *Did he hear the rattling of the chair legs?* The janitor wondered and waited for what seemed like an eternity. Finally, the steps continued until the sound of the Marine's movements slowly faded out of earshot. Only when absolutely sure that it was safe did he peer outside again. The coast clear, he took his cleaning supply cart and hurried on out.

***

Boris couldn't keep his eyes off Tatiana that night. As they walked up the front steps of the Bolshoi Theatre, he wasn't the only one. Removing his wife's fur overcoat inside, he was captivated by the dark red silk ballgown she wore. Classy, yet just revealing enough to dare a man to give her a long second glance. She paired her outfit with a tasteful diamond necklace that she said belonged to her great grandmother.

Twenty minutes before the performance began, they first said hello to his comrades from the office and their respective wives. Tatiana had over the years become good friends with some of these women as

Boris made his way up the bureaucratic ladder.

"There's someone I've wanted you to meet for a long time," he beamed, grabbing her hand. "Come on."

He led her through the crowd and up a flight of red carpeted stairs. Along the way, they passed a squabble of greybeards with their chests full of medals clanking against each other. Up ahead, a circle of people stood off to the side of a portrait depicting Catherine the Great. Their attention was focused on a man standing in the center. Boris and Tatiana squeezed their way through the gathering and towards him. No taller than 5'9 and balding at the top of his head, he gave no allusion of being the charismatic type. However, there was much more to this man from Stavropel—a man who excelled in outmaneuvering his opponents and ultimately gaining the trust of his General Secretary.

"Comrade Gorbachev, I would like to introduce you to my wife. Tatiana, Mikhail Gorbachev, Secretary of the Central Committee."

"It is a pleasure to meet you Mrs. Aleexev. I must say your husband is a blessed man. It must be difficult for him to stay and work the hours he does for me with a woman such as you waiting for him at home."

He was much different than the rest of his colleagues on the Politburo. As he reached out and shook her hand, she noted how much younger he looked than General Secretary Andropov and the rest. His face, adorned with a port-wine mark at the top of his forehead, did not seem cold, bombastic, or tired. There was, in fact, a general warmth and outgoingness about him that she observed.

After a few more moments of chatting, the couple politely excused themselves and made their way to their seats. The Russian ballet classic, 'Raymonda,' was about to begin. Tatiana's friends had gushed all week about seeing rising star Irek Mukhamedov dance on stage.

An hour and a half later, the curtain dropped. Intermission. Outside in the halls amongst the idle chatter, Tatiana spotted Alexei and Anastasia Gromokyo across the room. They had met once several months ago at a function similar to this. More importantly, though, Alexei's name was on the list.

She strolled over to the couple while Boris used the men's room. After exchanging pleasantries, Alexei was pulled into a conversation about the Red Army hockey team and their play at the recent Winter Olympics, leaving the two ladies to chat alone.

"So Tatiana, how are the boys? Last I recall your oldest is playing hockey himself?"

"*Da*. A good wing. Made two goals in his game last Saturday. Boris is so proud of him. I think he dreams of Nikita starring on that Olympic team one day. Has your husband had time to watch your little Matvei play his games lately?"

"*Net*. He has been busy working late for the last two weeks."

"Oh?"

"Leadership meetings," she said in almost a hushed whisper as she moved closer. "You might have already heard, but Andropov isn't exactly in the best health."

Tatiana nodded as the woman continued.

"Well, some already are looking to see who will take his place should something happen."

"Really? You'll have to excuse me, but I had no idea. Even married to a Kremlin official, I don't always keep up with everything." Tatiana was doing her best airhead impersonation. She'd learned early on in her career that it was best to play naïve lest she raise any suspicions. Boris had come home several times commenting on how tired and worn out Andropov appeared. "Tell me, who do you suspect would take over if something should happen?"

The woman seemed shocked that Tatiana knew so little, before giving a somewhat condescending smile. "Gorbachev, possibly. The other name mentioned is of course Chernenko."

"Oh! That means Boris would be an assistant to the General Secretary himself."

"Possibly." The woman abruptly excused herself and walked away speedily to another group of people. Tatiana sensed however that something was off. *She seemed almost ready to confide in me. As if she thought I were part of an exclusive circle. But why?*

***

"So, what did you think of Gorbachev?"

"Definitely not as old-looking as the rest of those on the Politburo," Tatiana retorted. Boris was sitting up in bed, reading a book as she finished with her evening skin routine.

"Anastasia says he might one day be General Secretary," Tatiana continued. "What do you think about all that?"

Boris looked up from the book. "It's a possibility. The older the General Secretary gets, the closer we all are to a new one."

"But if he did become the most powerful man in all of the Soviet Union, would you be happy? I mean, you would be in an even more prestigious role as his assistant."

He shrugged his shoulders and smiled. "That I wouldn't mind, I guess."

"You guess?! I figured you would have a bit more enthusiasm," she said as she turned off the light in the bathroom and came to bed.

"What are you, Lady Macbeth?" he said with a chuckle. "I prefer to focus on the present. Such as right now, I have plenty of enthusiasm for you in that silky nightgown."

After nine years of marriage, she could tell when he was holding back his real thoughts. Yes, that one-track mind of his was probably distracting him now. Still, there was something he wasn't saying to her.

"Oh, you do? Well..." she said as she climbed onto the bed and crawled up next to him. Placing a hand on his thigh, Tatiana slowly exhaled into his right ear. Boris's own breathing increased at this.

"Before I turn off this lamp, I'd like to know just why you aren't excited."

"Oh, I am."

"No, silly. I mean about one day becoming the personal assistant to the General Secretary."

He closed his eyes and sighed. She could tell he was trying to choose his words carefully.

"He's a good man, Tatiana. Understand that. My own personal feelings though are that we must stay the course in the ways of Lenin and the revolution. Attempting reform could carry severe consequences. There's more at stake than just the pursuit of the New Soviet man. Too great a change and you risk a country like Poland or East Germany getting ideas. Ideas that could spread like a disease and infect the Warsaw Pact. The Soviet Union would then cease to exist, and life as we know it would become chaos.

"So why work for him then if you feel so strongly? Why not just try to get a position with another official?"

He reached around with his arm and drew her close in a warm embrace. "Lots of reasons. Mainly though, because I think that the best way to make an impact is to be close to those not only in power, but those who you have fundamental disagreements with." He looked down at her, resting her head against his chest. "Does that make sense?"

She looked up and their eyes locked. Little did he realize that what he spoke of was the very thing she was doing each day.

"It does," she said as she took her left hand and placed it on his cheek tenderly. You're smart and persuasive Boris. I know you'll be a steady voice of reason whatever seat of power he's in."

She pulled his mouth to hers as their lips locked in a long, slow kiss.

"Tatiana," he said, coming up for air, "Only with you can I confide like this and feel safe. I love you."

She had long ago learned to detach herself, looking at all of this as just a job. Her relationship to Boris, the life she lived, all of it. But as much as she tried, there were still moments like this. Moments where, despite a duty to her country, she felt like a soulless android. She had this man's heart completely, yet she must use it however needed. *Block it out*, she urged herself. *What about James? You owe it to him to stay focused and solve this mess. Don't let up now.*

She leaned in and kissed him deeply once more before reaching to turn off the lamp.

"I   love   you   too."

8

The Seventh Day

Few were aware of the pistol range tucked into the basement of the U.S. Embassy. Whereas the Marines frequented it often to maintain their marksmanship skills, the CIA's officers did so on an irregular basis. The prevailing mindset had been that if one was to avoid killing a Russian on Soviet soil (and starting WWIII), then it was far better to focus on perfecting tradecraft rather than hitting a target with a handgun.

Josh O'Neil, however, didn't subscribe to this train of thought. Three times a week, the Deputy Chief of Station would walk down through the sparsely illuminated corridors to practice from the second to last lane on the right. He'd more than just qualified with a .45 automatic during his days at Quantico. In fact, he'd once been a regular finalist at the national championships held at Camp Perry in Ohio. Nowadays, he trained with a .22 Ruger Mark II automatic, preferring the way it handled.

It was on this afternoon that he'd found his boss eager to join him. Carson, once a fair shot himself, knew there was some rust that needed shaking off. It had been almost two months since the COS last used a firearm. Even if he was supposed to leave the action to the younger members of Moscow Station, he felt a desire to be ready for anything.

"Alright Chief, let's start with the .45," O'Neil said as he set the small lockbox on a table just outside the lanes. Taking out the pistol, he handed it to Carson, who pulled the slide back to check that it was unloaded. O'Neil then handed him a loaded clip, which the COS inserted and then step towards lane five.

Cooper pulled the slide back with his left hand, chambering the first round and waited.

"You're on!"

A light above a silhouette target twenty yards away came on, and Carson took aim. He rapidly dispensed with all five of his rounds before lowering the .45. *I've got to do better than that.*

An electric pulley brought the target forward to judge. O'Neil stepped next to Carson to examine it.

"Solid shooting for a first time in a while," the Deputy remarked. "All five on paper, three in the black, and two in the chest."

"Yes but I was prepared and ready to fire. If I were out in the field, I wouldn't necessarily have time to think. Let's go again."

O'Neil nodded and got his boss another clip and target. *Probably just wants to set a good example for the rest of us. He can't really be serious.* It struck him as somewhat odd that Cooper, old as he was and the COS of Moscow Station to boot, could imagine a scenario where he'd be in a firefight.

After so many years in the field however, Cooper wasn't ready to let it go. He could recall at least three occasions where his ability to fire a gun better than the next guy had saved his life. He knew what everyone from the top brass at Langley down to even his Deputy COS thought. He didn't care. Deep down, Carson Cooper believed there was still one more time. One more time when decisiveness and marksmanship would be required.

By his own standards, he was in need of more time at the range. Cooper knew plenty of younger guys, including O'Neil, that were better. But he was determined to return to form. *Then, I'll be ready.*

Nearly an hour later, Cooper and O'Neil headed back to the station where a young case officer was waiting to give the COS some news.

"He's up and disappeared' the young man said after completing his summary. "That's what they're saying."

Cooper brushed his index finger along his mustache. "So, we still have a chance then."

The case officer shook his head. His agents at Lubyanka reported that the search for the missing traitor was still ongoing. "Sir, I'd rather look for a needle in a haystack. If the KGB doesn't know where he is, how should we expect to find him?"

"We don't. He'll find us instead."

"What?"

"Son, Torchlight is a highly-skilled and experienced counterintelligence officer. He knows each and every next move the KGB will take against him. That's evident by their frustration. Now, his only move, if he wants to get out of this alive, is to come to us. We're his only lifeline. You following so far?"

The officer nodded.

"He could be wary and think it's a trap, or he could miss seeing it altogether, but I want a signal made for a meeting. If he responds, we move carefully and plan to make contact."

"If he doesn't?"

Cooper knew that scenario was likely. He never liked being told the odds, though. One way or another, he believed Torchlight would find them.

Four miles away, Ivanovich was doing his best to find the silver lining in his new living accommodations: squatting in an abandoned textile factory. The Major was thankful for this particular roof over his head. The KGB were unlikely to pay a visit here. Food wasn't an issue either—though not as luxurious as what he'd become used to buying from the closed stores serving the *nomenklatura*. He'd always been resourceful and never struggled to meet a necessity for himself.

Walking along the ghostly factory floor, he carried with him a loaf of bread and some vodka. Ivanovich would have it in the manager's office, which overlooked the discarded machinery. He did his best to clean this space up and make it somewhat livable. Inside, he had a table, a badly worn sofa, and two sets of factory clothes that he'd changed into.

It had only been a week, yet it felt much longer. He feared for the safety of his family. He also was concerned for the fate of the reform-minded Politburo member.

Somehow I've got to make a move. If I stay here, everything else I care about will be destroyed. There has to be a way...

***

Colonel Oleg Naumov was a man on a clear trajectory for success. Recently honored for successfully pinpointing the source of leaks within research and development at Moscow University, he was a rising star at Lubyanka. Many believed that though he was only forty, he could become chairman of the KGB one day. No assignment had yet proven too big a challenge for him. As such, he was unfazed when ordered to report the office of the Chief of the 2nd Directorate. Making his way from his desk to the head of the KGB's counterintelligence division, he tried to guess at what this next assignment might be.

Naumov entered the room to find the Chief seated behind an old dusty desk that appeared to originate from the age of czars. He seemed to be in deep concentration while reading the contents of the file folder before him.

"You asked to see me, Chief of Directorate?"

"Comrade, the Soviet Union has recently made a significant breakthrough in its efforts to stop the treacherous actions of the American Imperialists. By way of assets within their very Embassy, we've obtained information that will lead to the arrest of many spies here in Moscow.

"Our chairman is eager to identify these traitors. That is why I have decided that you will be in charge of the investigation."

"It's an honor that you've chosen me for this

assignment," replied Naumov.

"I've no doubts that you'll do well. Now, the stolen communication files from the U.S. Embassy we obtained seem to provide clues and in some cases names, to both CIA officers and the agents they run. Those we don't know yet, find out who they are. Use your best judgment in deciding when to move in on them and begin arrests. Once you start, you'll have to move quickly lest the Americans realize what's happening. Is that understood?"

Ten minutes later, Naumov had returned to his office and was eagerly reading the first pages of the file. It was incredible. For the longest time, American intelligence operations were thought to have made little headway in the Soviet capital. This new trove of intel dispelled any fantasies that such a reality still existed. Over the last several years, the Americans had infiltrated key areas including defense R&D, the Kremlin and the KGB through the recruitment of agents at the highest levels. Now, it would be his job to bring the traitors to justice and reaffirm the KGB's superiority.

Turning the pages, one suspect caught his attention. The communication from the CIA's Moscow Station suspiciously left out quite a bit of detail regarding the agent. What it did describe, though, was a person code-named "SHROUD" that had obtained intel from the highest echelons of the Kremlin, specifically Politburo meetings and actions, through a close relation working there .

It could take many months though to narrow this suspect from all close family members of the high-ranking Kremlin nomenklatura. We don't have that kind of time.

He continued to pore over the intel further until an idea came to mind—an idea that he was sure would lead him to this mysterious spy.

9

The Eighth Day

It was a beautiful day for a stroll in the historic Old Town Market Place. Here in the oldest part of Warsaw, tourists and shoppers bustled amongst the 17th and 18th-century merchant houses colored in various pastels which surrounded the square. At the center of the square stood a bronze fountain of a mermaid. Macy Holden couldn't have asked for a better day to get out of the diplomatic compound with her toddler.

She pushed her son in his stroller while purchasing vegetables in the marketplace. She looked at her watch. Only a couple more minutes until game time.

Macy and her husband Ron were an ideal couple for the world of espionage, if only because they were the last people you would expect. Before joining the State Department, Ron had worked for a travel agency for several years and later moved into middle management. His job here focused officially on cultural exchanges, as well as helping to get tickets to special events for employees at the Embassy. Macy, meanwhile, was your ordinary American housewife, taking care of her kid and appearing enamored with living in Europe. The two had fallen into regular routines rather quickly, and counterintelligence services had grown lax in their surveillance of them.

Macy took full advantage of it. There was no need for a disguise. A stroller gave her an easy excuse to carry and hide whatever packages she might have. Ron often had to remind her not to take so many risks. She was eager, however, and had no intention of slowing down.

Out of the corner of her eye, she saw him—grey coat, black dress shoes, slightly overweight, and wearing glasses while standing by the fountains. Game time.

"Excuse me," she said in English as she approached him, "do you happen to know where I can get good fresh fish? The vendor I always like to buy from has already sold out."

"There's a shop not far from here off of *Musial*. They rarely sell out, but their salmon is quite tasty."

All good, she said to herself. He'd given the correct code word. "They want to know about any unusual recent activity, particularly involving the KGB," she said as she shook his hand, playing up the outward appearance of a naïve American housewife to anyone watching.

"Why?"

"No particular reason. Do you know of any sleeper cells that may be on the move?"

The SB officer, part of the Polish secret police, smiled and gushed over the toddler in the stroller. "He's going to grow up to be something special one day. You can always tell just by looking at that sparkle in their eye. He has that look."

'To answer your question," he continued, "there are several individuals who we're told to avoid and not interfere with by orders of the KGB. All of whom are young men working in either factories or other similar positions. Why we're to stay away from them is a mystery to all within the SB."

"So if they were up to something, nobody would know?"

"I didn't say that. A couple years ago, when the CIA first approached me, I thought it worth keeping tabs on those assets. As it so happens, three of them have disappeared.

"Disappeared?"

"Didn't show up to work, haven't been seen going to or from their apartments—it's like they never existed."

"And you don't know where they went?"

"My guess is as good as yours."

The meeting ended shortly thereafter. Any more than two minutes seen with an American diplomat's wife and the excuse that he was helping a confused woman find her way around town wouldn't go over well with his bosses. Macy continued on her way, pushing the stroller, pondering what it all meant and where those sleeper agents could be.

***

The dacha wasn't much to look at. It was in desperate need of a new coat of paint, and two of its shutters had fallen off. Jozef Woźniak didn't mind. After nearly a week of sitting in the back of unmarked trucks, he was glad just to finally reach his destination in the newly created Losiny Ostrov National Park. He took in the pleasant scent of the surrounding pine trees as heard the sound of birds chirping. *This would be as good a place as any to prepare for the mission.*

He stepped onto the dacha's oak wood porch and knocked on a wide-framed green door. A man about the same age, height, and build as him soon came to see who was standing outside.

"Yes?"

"Warsaw sends its cold compliments," he replied.

"Come in."

Inside, five more KGB Spetsnaz members sat in front of a fireplace, telling jokes, and cleaning their PSS pistols.

"I think you're the last one," said the man whose name was Arkady. "I'll radio and let the commander know we're ready. Food's in the kitchen if you want any."

Woźniak returned a minute later with a full plate to see General Dmitri Medved standing in front of the door removing his officer's coat. Immediately, the young man set his plate down and saluted the general.

"At ease, comrade. It's good to see you. I know it's been a long journey for you and everyone else here. Eat up." Having the room's full attention, Medved turned and addressed them all.

"Comrades, each of you has been activated out of deep cover. You've put on a mask so that one day you might come up from the shadows to strike a major blow for your country. Now, comrades, the time has come.

"Before you finished your training and departed Moscow, you were briefed of the future intent concerning your mission. Some minor details have shifted, but the overall objective has not: to eliminate any threat to our system of government with deadly precision. Do not forget who you are. As members of the KGB, you are the sword and shield of the Rodina."

One of the men spoke up. "General, who is it that we're targeting?"

"A man from Stavropol who secretly despises the Soviet way of life. A man who sits on the Politburo and has tricked our great General Secretary: Mikhail Gorbachev."

***

Chinski Rabinovich, had no idea that he was being watched. He would have kept his hand inside his right pocket if he'd realized a KGB colonel was watching him from a third floor, street view window.

"Comrade Gusev, are your men in position?" Colonel Naumov whispered into a hand radio while looking through his binoculars.

"They're stationed at each end of the street, as well as inside the apartment lobbies running alongside. There's no way anyone can escape Colonel."

"Very good. Here he comes now."

A tall, wiry man turned onto the street and started towards their position. Besides giving an extra glance at his surroundings, he gave no cause for suspicion.

Rabinovich, eventually came to a park bench and sat

down. Taking a newspaper he carried under his arm, he opened it and began to read. Pedestrians came and went, but none seemed to distract him from the headlines.

A much younger officer standing next to Naumov glanced at his watch, hoping his boss wouldn't notice.

"Comrade, are we growing impatient?"

"No, not all Colonel," he sheepishly replied like a student caught gazing at the clock behind his desk.

"Good. It is best then that you keep attentive to the operation at hand, unless you'd like to be cited for neglecting your responsibilities in my report."

Just then, the suspect reached into his coat pocket and drew out a handkerchief to blow his nose. As he did, something fell to the ground.

"Did anyone else see what he dropped?"

"It's hard to tell Colonel, but it appears to be a small rock."

"When he moves away, I want one team to follow and arrest him quietly. The other team will stay and see who retrieves whatever the thing is. That is an order!"

Five minutes later, the man on the bench finally stood up, newspaper in hand, and walked away. Just as ordered, a team followed and arrested him a block away.

"What is this? My name is Chinski Rabinovich, and I'm an engineer at Gagarin Aerospace Laboratory. I'm expected back at work in five minutes."

"We will notify your Director, comrade. If you would please come with us, we have some questions to ask. That is all we can say at this time. It is a matter of state security."

Gulag in Siberia or a swift execution—the man did not know. The only certainty was that life as he knew it had just ended.

"Patience, comrades. The contact will soon arrive."

It took two hours, but the contact did arrive. A middle-aged woman sat down at the bench with her purse and rested as if she'd been walking quite a long way. Reaching down to rub her ankles, she adjusted the black high-heel shoes she wore.

"There, Colonel, she's taken the object dropped by the suspect."

"All teams move in at once. Let's take her in and see what's inside that rock."

They ran towards her from three directions. There was no escape or warning. The first officer to reach her slammed the woman fully onto the bench, pinning her down as he began to place handcuffs on her. What screaming the suspect did was both quick and muffled as she was promptly dragged into a car and hauled off to Lubyanka.

10

It took but six hours for the woman to break. Theresa Medvedev, the wife of an automobile manufacturing plant director, confessed to her interrogator that she'd been recruited four years earlier by another woman whom she met but three times. Her job was that of a courier, passing along notes and packages from dead drops.

Theresa's recruiter? A young woman, looking to be in her early thirties with dark hair and glasses and a beauty mark on her left cheek. *Probably a disguise*, pondered a frustrated Naumov. *If it's a CIA officer, the physical description is nearly worthless.* The suspect's primary contact, however, was through a man working at a restaurant inside a prominent hotel. They'd gotten his full description and made plans to arrest him within the next few hours.

"Colonel, we've yet to get a confession from the suspect who left the package," announced an officer entering Naumov's office.

"Keep at it for a couple more hours. Then send him to a cell to be awakened and questioned again at whatever random hours you choose. We will break him lieutenant."

Naumov returned to the file before him as the subordinate left. Already there were plans in place for two more stings the following day. He knew he would have to move swiftly if he were to sweep up as many

Imperialist spies as he could before the Americans realized what was happening.

But who was this woman that the spy had mentioned? A CIA officer? Another courier, or an agent? *There's no way of telling. Not yet at least.* And there was still the question of the unnamed spy sending information from the Kremlin via a close relation. He would have to continue digging.

***

Tatiana couldn't sleep. As Boris snored loudly beside her in bed, she thought about the past—about The Farm, volunteering for the non-official cover operation, and first meeting her husband.

Audrey Davis was recruited straight out of college. Had she not chosen the career path of a spy, she may have gone on to be a history professor, settled down, and eventually become a stay-at-home mom. Nonetheless, the young woman eager to see the world excelled in her training and impressed the CIA instructors. Initially, it was to be a standard diplomatic posting in Eastern Europe, before a unique volunteer opportunity arose.

Tatiana recalled how they described it. A chance to potentially be one of the most effective spies the Agency ever had. But, there would be sacrifices. Sacrifices that initially chilled her to the bone. *Set a honey trap to marry a Russian that worked inside the Kremlin? Doubt anyone else from the Tri Delta house did that after college.* Only a handful of people would ever know her identity. Length of the mission? Seven years minimum.

Why did I ever say yes? Then she remembered. The thrill of adventure was a part of it, but there was much more. *It was following in Dad's footsteps.* It was also a chance to escape the sadness at home her father, a CIA paramilitary operations officer, left behind after being killed in Vietnam.

Boris suddenly rolled into her, still asleep, interrupting her thoughts. She gently pushed him back to his side of the bed.

The Agency had never explicitly intended for Boris to be her husband. He was merely one of many potential targets. They first met years ago at an unofficial Party gathering celebrating the birthday of a Central Committee member. She'd caught his eye from across the room. When he finally approached her, she had him hooked.

Where was she from? She told him her name was Tatiana Savchenkov. Born near the end of The Great Patriotic War in Ukraine to a Russian family, she was orphaned before it was over. Her only relative still alive, an older cousin, had raised her. Now she worked as a flight attendant and had been invited here by a mutual acquaintance.

The two talked and flirted for hours. Boris, quickly falling head over heels, told her all about his new job at the Kremlin just after graduating from Moscow University. A perfect pairing, to the CIA's liking at least. Three months later, they were engaged.

A year into their marriage, the doctor told her she was expecting. When Nikita was born, she fell in love with him. The same went for Sergei. Her two sons had now become the most important people in her life.

Boris's arm swung out and almost hit her square in the face. *He's always a restless sleeper.* Tatiana took his right arm now resting atop her chest and pushed it aside. This finally woke him up.

"Everything okay? How long have you been sitting up like that?"

She could see the genuine look of concern on his face.

"Oh, I'm fine. Just having a little trouble sleeping."

"I wasn't snoring again, was I?"

"No," she said, smiling slightly. "Not this time."

"You know, this isn't the first time I've seen you like this."

"Really?"

He nodded. "Normally I'd fall back asleep. But when I really think about it, lying there awake, you always look deep in thought about something."

"Maybe."

"Can always share with me. I'm a good listener sometimes. Try me," he said, squeezing her hand.

"You never met my father."

"No. You said your parents died when you're young. During the war."

"*Da*, it's just, sometimes I think about him. I can't really talk about it, but I do remember him. For much of my life, I've done without him. Lately, it's just...I wonder what it would be like to have him in my life now, in the lives of his grandchildren."

"I bet he would have loved them. Watching them skate on the ice scoring goals in the winter, running and climbing on everything in the woods in the summer."

"You really think so?"

"Absolutely."

She kissed him slowly. "You're right. I think I'm going to try to go back to sleep now."

"You sure you're good?"

"I'm okay. Goodnight honey."

She turned and faced the other side of the bed and pretended to sleep. Boris meanwhile settled back and began to snore once more. As he did she thought again about it all. What if she returned? What sort of life would await her? What about Nikita and Sergei? What would happen to them? She couldn't leave them.

She knew that she couldn't keep this up forever. A time would come when she'd be forced to make a move. *But what will happen to the kids? Will they really be able to adjust to a life in the West?*

The answer would have to wait, however, as she closed her eyes and drifted off into a deep sleep.

***

Two hours late. The short man with red cheeks was freezing and ready to go home. Even for a Muscovite, this was a cold winter evening. Trying to figure what had happened to her would only be speculation. He needed to let his handler know that he wouldn't have the package for her tomorrow.

The place where he was supposed to leave the signal was about three blocks away: two chalk lines on the side of a butcher shop door next to a premier grammar school. By the time he got home, it would be almost midnight, he grumbled. He took his job seriously however and wouldn't have dared thought of leaving earlier.

It was two years ago when he met his CIA handler. He could still recall every detail of how he passed a note to an American Embassy official as they were leaving the lobby of the Leningradskaya hotel. Money was not the motivating factor, but rather a genuine passion for Western ideals and personal liberties.

Working as a waiter, he had overheard a conversation between two defense ministry officials too drunk to use any discretion while discussing operation plans for Afghanistan. He wrote down all that he heard from memory and added that other top officials frequented the restaurant often.

After three long months, Langley verified the information and permitted Moscow Station to set up a meeting. Right away, it was determined that he would pass all information he received to a woman that often visited his restaurant with her friends for lunch. He learned fast how to pass notes under glasses, napkins, and plates without being noticed. Soon, he became one of the CIA's most trusted agents.

Her name he'd learned was Tatiana Aleexev, the wife of a personal aide to Politburo member Mikhail

Gorbachev. He found her incredibly attractive and a time or two had daydreamed about her. Not that it would ever go anywhere. Never did she engage in any banter with him when he waited on her table, keeping her remarks cordial and on the meal.

Over time, she would slip notes to him as well, giving him directions to act as a go-to of sorts for couriers with information the CIA needed. Now, with one of his couriers missing, he wondered what she would think.

Finally, he reached the point where the signal was to be made. Without stopping he drew two quick marks with a stick of chalk along a wall and kept going. He couldn't figure out why she wanted the mark here. Must be along her way to the hotel, he finally guessed.

Nearly an hour later, he finally made it to his apartment building. Exhausted, he'd take a quick shower and then make a late dinner once inside. He began to fumble with his keys as he neared his doorway when he noticed something strange. There were muddy footprints appearing to lead inside. He hadn't requested any repairs. A sick feeling sat inside his stomach. Instinctively turning around, no sooner had he reached the elevator when several men in overcoats rushed towards him. A move towards the stairway was in vain as they tackled him to the ground.

"The colonel will be happy to see this one. Take him away."

***

Ivanovich saw the signal. The blinds in the third-floor apartment just ahead were opened, shut and opened in the right way, manner and pattern. *But is it real?*

For all he knew, someone else had been arrested and forced to talk. Even if it wasn't a trap, how could he trust the Americans if they said surveillance was clear when it really wasn't?

No, it's too dangerous to go. Best to keep looking for another way   to   make   contact.

11

The Ninth Day

"Nikita, remember your hockey bag. How many times have I told you?"

"Yes, mom."

"I'll see you both this afternoon. Love you two."

Tatiana began to pull away from the curb as Sergei waved goodbye and headed inside with his older brother. If she hadn't been looking in the rearview mirror to see him wave, she would've missed the two chalk marks streaked alongside a wall right next to the school.

Strange. I'll have to report that to Cooper. Tatiana continued on her way. She was supposed to stop by her friend Fiona's and pick her up before joining the rest of their friends for lunch at the hotel.

Fiona Churkin lived not far away in an apartment similar to hers. Fiona's husband happened to be a naval officer stationed with the Baltic fleet commanding a Yankee class nuclear submarine. Every so often, a random tidbit Commander Churkin mentioned to his wife and repeated to her was worth relaying to Langley.

"Tatiana! How are you this morning? Do come in," the woman said. "How are the children doing today?"

"Just fine. Nikita has a playoff hockey game tomorrow and can't stop talking about it."

The two went into the living area where a pot of coffee was ready to be poured, along with a plate of shortbread cookies. For a while they made idle chatter, when there was a knock at the door. Fiona excused herself to go answer it.

"Dmitri! What brings you here, brother?"

"I had some free time this morning and figured I would stop by to visit."

The two gave each other a quick hug and returned to the living area. "Tatiana, I would like you to meet my brother, General Dmitri Medved."

From the list!

"It is a pleasure to meet you, General," she said as she reached out to shake hands.

"The pleasure is all mine," he said, taking her extended hand and kissing it somewhat dramatically.

Fiona continued. "Dmitri, Tatiana's husband, Boris Alexeev, is a personal aide to Mikhail Gorbachev."

A flash in his eyes flickered but for a moment. "Really? Your husband, no doubt, has a great responsibility serving a voting member of our powerful Politburo."

"I would agree, General."

"Please call me Dimitri. General is only for my subordinates," he said while gazing at her.

As the three visited, Tatiana's focus was somewhere else. This KGB General could be a lifeline to figuring out this list. She couldn't waste this opportunity. The only question now was how to do it.

"Didn't you go out with that woman from the University last week? What was her name?"

"Ah, don't bring her up. She was rather dull, to be frank, Fiona. All she spoke about over dinner was physics and her four cats at home." He looked over at Tatiana flirtatiously and then said, "I guess all the exciting ones are already married."

Fiona, failing to catch the meaning of that remark, continued peppering her brother with questions about his love life. All the while, Dmitri passively answered while making eyes at her guest.

Finally, when his sister had left the room to get another cup of coffee, he made his move.

"I'm having a dinner party at my dacha out near Elk Island next Friday. Why don't you come? You could even get there early and I could show you some of the horses in the stable. Tell your husband that you're visiting with Fiona that evening."

She looked into the glassy green eyes and saw a man that had but one thing on his mind. She knew this was her perfect chance if she played this right.

"Mmm, maybe. I'm not sure what your intentions are," she with a sultry expression.

"There's only one way to find out. Say yes," he implored.

Tatiana could hear her friend leaving the kitchen.

"I'll be there at 3."

***

"My name is Nicholas Baryshnikov. I work as a waiter at the Leningradskaya hotel. I know nothing about any spying."

It had been twelve hours and Naumov still had yet to get a confession from the waiter. The others had caved once the right buttons were pushed. The Colonel had no doubt it would be the same with this one.

"Comrade Baryshnikov, you can continue these repeated lies if you would like. However, you should know that it won't get any easier making them."

"I have said all there is."

"Very well." With that, Naumov exited the room. "You know what to do," he said to two guards outside.

Both men nodded and then stepped inside the holding room. The Colonel had not even made it halfway down the hall when he heard screams of agony come from Baryshnikov's lungs.

***

"Thank you," Tatiana said as she was handed a menu at the restaurant. She was perplexed to see that their table was being waited on by a different server.

First the signal, now he's not here. What's going on?

***

Carson was in disbelief. *What were the odds? Five agents now missing.* It was the single biggest hit the

99

CIA's Moscow Station had taken in its entire history.

Sitting at his desk, he tossed the baseball into the air. Forty-plus years serving his country, and it couldn't just come down to this. *Not this way.* Some were itching for the chance to put him out to pasture. He wasn't ready. Not by a longshot. It had been all he'd known since he'd graduated from Yale. While all his friends choose a path that led to Wall Street or a prestigious law firm, he chose the one less traveled for an Ivy Leaguer at a time before Pearl Harbor. His father pitched a fit when he learned that he'd joined the army and was to be a 2nd Lieutenant. "You're really going to throw your life away like this? Do you think you can really be happy making squat in the army? What for? There isn't a war going on! Even if there was, why get your head shot at?"

Because a war is coming. Maybe you can't see the storm clouds gathering, but I won't sit in a cushy office and not act.

His dad never understood. But it didn't matter. Carson quickly found purpose and meaning in the work he did for a special division of Army intelligence, known only to a few as The Veracruz Branch. Founded by then Chairman of the Joint Chiefs of Staff General Douglas MacArthur, they led the way in clandestine operations before the OSS and before the CIA.

The missions he'd undertaken, the Embassies where he'd been stationed, the agents he'd run—he could be a millionaire if he were allowed to tell his stories. Not that he'd ever would, of course. It had been a good life. His only regret was that he wished he could've spent more time with his wife. For thirty-seven years, Cathy never once complained about his work, always kind with a big heart. He missed her every day.

How do you keep your officers from being killed and your agents from being arrested? How do you find an agent that's on the run but holds the answers to everything? How do you stay in the game just a little longer before they call you home? Just how do you, Carson?

He needed to get out of this windowless, vaulted office and get a breath of fresh air. Taking his jacket, he locked up and headed out to the garage. Cooper hopped into a black Mercedes diplomats' car he'd the keys to and drove out past the Marine guarded gate and onto the street.

Changing gears, he realized that this was the first time since he arrived that morning at Sheremetyevo that he'd been behind the wheel. He rolled down the driver's window to let in some cold air. It felt good for once to be out on the street and on the move rather than simply reacting to problems from behind a desk.

A light appeared on the dashboard. *Where did they say the gas station was again?* He remembered what O'Neil had told him about the spot most of the diplomats used and headed that way.

***

Ivanovich was also out and about that evening. It was a clear sky, and the wind had died down some. Too good of weather to stay hidden inside the factory. Up ahead was the diplomats' gas station, but he paid it no mind as he walked along the sidewalk. A black Mercedes drove up from behind and past beside him. The license plates, identifying the car as belonging to the American Embassy, grabbed his attention. His gazed was transfixed on the vehicle as it turned into the station.

A thought immediately came to mind. It was crazy, yet it might be his only real chance. Scanning the street, he saw he was in the black and made his move.

***

Cooper's eyes appeared transfixed on the rapidly changing numbers on the pump as he waited until his tank was full. He was still lost in thought, trying to figure out a solution to the whole mess and wondering what Langley would say. His guard momentarily let down. Behind his back, on the other side of the car, approached Ivanovich, hastily scribbling a note of some kind.

Suddenly the garish sound of a car backfiring echoed from down the street. Cooper instinctively turned around and saw the guilty party was a Volvo 760 belonging to a Swedish Embassy official. It was in that next moment that he saw his most wanted man: Torchlight with a hand caught reaching in through the driver's window. Their eyes locking, the two stared at one another in a mixture of fear and disbelief.

"Hey, can I help you?" It was the first thing that came out of Carson's mouth. How lucky he felt now to have had an opportunity to view a photograph of the KGB officer before his arrival.

Ivanovich stood frozen in panic. He had no idea

he was speaking to the Chief of Moscow Station, much less a member of the CIA. All he wanted now was to give him the note and disappear fast, lest he be seen. A station attendant leaned against a doorway nearby, apparently indifferent to both, if he were really preoccupied with the magazine he seemed to be reading.

"I…I have something for your Embassy. Please see that it gets to your Ambassador." He paused before continuing in a hushed voice. "It's important. My life is in danger. I need help."

Carson took stock of their surroundings and then spoke before Torchlight could run. "Listen, I know who you are. I'm going to continue filling up my tank while you're going to walk on down the street. Cool, calm like nothing is going on. Be at that corner there by the time I make my turn back home. Understood?"

Ivanovich nodded and moved along as Cooper turned back to the pump. He didn't see anyone watching them, but it was dark and he couldn't be completely sure. There was another factor that played through the Chief of Station's mind. What if Torchlight had been turned or was being used by them? If they were and he tried anything, it would be over in an instant. *What would keep them from killing me like they did Shephard?*

You can't live in fear, Carson. Let it paralyze you, and it will make all the wrong decisions for you. He got back in the car and turned the ignition. If he didn't take this chance, Langley could very well shut down all operations, put the station on ice, and send him on the next flight to Dulles International.

Pulling out of the parking lot, Carson realized that he only had about twenty seconds to make a decision before reaching the corner. The COS said his own silent prayer. "If any of you lacks wisdom, you should ask God, who gives generously to all without finding fault." This was the verse he often recalled in difficult times of uncertainty.

Ivanovich was right where he told him to be. Hastily, he leaned over to open the passenger door as he slowly rounded the corner. "Get in!"

He didn't need to be told twice. Torchlight hopped in and pulled the door shut. Cooper took his head and pushed the man onto the floor as he sped away.

"Whatever you do, don't get up."

Five minutes away from the Embassy. He looked in his rearview but saw not a single KGB or militiaman. *Still doesn't mean they're not out there.*

Neither said a word as the car drove. In light of all that had recently transpired, both thought it'd be a miracle if they actually made it back.

Cooper could see the Embassy gates straight ahead. The customary militiaman was standing by to survey all who came and went. He'd for sure notice Torchlight crouched between the seat and the dashboard.

Taking his jacket off, he threw it over his passenger. The Mercedes slowed to a stop as the Marine walked up to the driver's window.

"Good evening, sir. Glad to have you back for the evening," the Sergeant said as he inspected Cooper's ID.

"Thanks. Y'all got a poker game going on later tonight? If so, I'm down to join."

"A couple of guys just might. I'll let them know you're coming."

The gates began to creak open as the militiaman's eyes peered his way. Cooper did his best to ignore them as he drove on through. He breathed a sigh of relief. As they entered the garage, there appeared to be no one around.

"Alright, Pyotr Ivanovich, you're now officially on U.S. territory. For the time being. Keep doing everything I say and don't do anything that may give the wrong signal, understood?"

"Yes. I will. Thank you for helping me."

Just as he pulled into his parking spot, two armed Marines came up to the car.

"Thanks guys," Carson said as he got out. We need to move him to a secure spot without anyone else seeing. Anyone got a blindfold?"

"I don't sir, but this could do just as well," said one of the Marines, a Corporal, as he removed his khaki colored tie and wrapped it around Torchlight's head, covering his eyes.

Cooper shook his head and grinned. Glad to be back safe and sound, he was ready to learn the truth about that infamous night along the Moskva.

12

O'Neil hurried downstairs to the floor where they were keeping Ivanovich. He'd had to leave dinner midway with his wife when he received word. Walking as fast as he could down the corridors of the Embassy, he stopped outside an unmarked door where a Marine stood guard. Upon verification of his ID, the Deputy Chief of Station entered the interrogation room.

"How in the world, Cooper, did you find this guy?" the deputy chief said, in near disbelief at seeing their agent alive and well.

"Literally fell into my lap—or so I think right now." Cooper recounted the story while Ivanovich devoured the warm dinner. Coffee and roast beef sandwiches had never tasted this good for the KGB officer.

The COS turned to the spy. "Alright Pyotr, tell us from the beginning what this is all about."

"You mean you never got my message?"

"No. Unfortunately, the cigarette carton containing your note was damaged while your case officer attempted to escape the KGB. The man you met with is now dead. All the more reason why we need answers now," said Cooper.

Ivanovich spent the next few minutes recounting

the details of the plot and what was at stake before O'Neil interjected.

"Why weren't you arrested that night? The KGB had that place pretty well covered. Did you know they'd been tipped off?"

"I don't know, but I'm thankful to have gotten out of there when I did. I've been on run since then and haven't returned home. You must understand, these people are powerful. They have the resources and capabilities to do what they want and learn what they want."

For the next four hours, they grilled Torchlight. No question went unasked and once was never enough. His story, however, remained unchanged.

"D—n, he's telling the truth alright," O'Neil said sleepily as they finally left the room.

"I know. I'm going to have to go wake Chris and get all this over to Langley ASAP."

"Still plenty of questions," said O'Neil. "We haven't a clue when they might try anything, or even who they'll use to carry out the hit. KGB, GRU, hired thugs, Eastern bloc secret police-type? There's just no telling."

"Yes, but we can still call this a win tonight," Cooper said with a yawn. "Tomorrow, Moscow Station kicks it into third gear."

***

Palmer reread the message a third time. It all seemed too unbelievable to fathom: multiple agents arrested prompting questions of a possible leak, and now Torchlight safe and sound at the Embassy.

"Doesn't get much crazier than that, does it, Dave?"

Palmer sat just across from the Director of the CIA. A man tasked with rebuilding the Agency, Director Casey hated the idea of standing down in the face of any sort of setbacks. He loathed even more James Shephard's death at the hands of an enemy who abruptly decided to forget the unwritten rules of espionage. If he had anything to say about it, they would strike back in decisive fashion.

"In thirty minutes, I'm supposed to leave for the White House to meet with the President. Before I do, what's your take?"

"Well, from the file we have on Gorbachev, he really could be the best chance we get at a Soviet leader who we could work with."

"Go on."

"Bill, when he was only six, this guy's grandfather got swept up in Stalin's great purge. They arrested and beat the old man pretty badly. The granddad never blamed Stalin, but what happened wasn't exactly a secret in his family. His wife also had family affected by the purges. There are even stories about how, in college, he openly questioned professors who would blindly quote Stalin, or how he stood up for Jewish friends that were singled out and bullied. This guy has the right sort of motives to come in and shake up the system. He's demonstrated all the tendencies of being a squeaky wheel. From reports we've gathered, including from Shroud, Andropov not only likes him a lot but is the reason Gorbachev became a Politburo member in the first place.

"On those grounds alone, he's a valuable asset not just to us, but to the free world itself. And to be clear, that's not hyperbole. If he gets a chance at power someday, he's someone the President could work with. We've got to find a way to keep him alive."

"Point well made," said the Director, "but how do you go about doing that? We can't just tell anyone in the Kremlin about this information. That has its own set of problems. Even if we told Andropov, he's liable to think we're only trying to stir the pot."

"So, recommend to Reagan that we keep digging. Don't stop because of the recent adversity. Once we have more intel, we can consider taking decisive action if needed."

"If we do, we can't just deploy a team of Navy Seals to Moscow and have them eliminate all threats to this guy's life."

"But what if we could stop these assassins before they make a move using what we already have on the ground? We know from a recent report in Warsaw that several KGB illegals are missing and likely have been activated. The pieces are getting connected. Our best asset is Moscow Station and the agents at its disposal.

"I'll give that to you, Dave. You were right to have them get that intel from the SB agent. Still way too many question marks though. I've decided to recommend a push for gathering more information on this while holding off on any tactical action."

"You think, sir, if necessary, would POTUS ever be open to intervening by lethal force to stop the assassination?"

The Director looked him straight in the eyes. "Given the fact he's serious about the Soviets and is the only serving President to survive being shot, I'd say he just might Palmer. He just might."

***

The Tenth Day

"Comrade Baryshnikov, you don't look so well. Would you care for some tea?"

It had been a rough thirty hours. Thirty-filled hours of beatings, sleep deprivation and questioning at random hours. Both of the waiter's eyes were purple, and his lips had swollen up. He was sure that he'd at least one broken rib, as he was barely able to stand on his own power. Yet, despite all of this, his captors had been unable to break his stubborn resolve. Every time he was questioned about his CIA contacts, he would feign ignorance, giving only his name and occupation.

Colonel Naumov poured a cup of tea for his prisoner and set it beside him. He watched him sip it slowly, as the Colonel lit himself a cigarette.

"I know what you are thinking," said Naumov. "They can't break me. They don't understand my cause. If they did, they would know what keeps me going."

He inhaled a puff before exhaling a cloud that hung over them both and continued.

"But I do, Nicholas. I understand. I get you want more than your current status in life. You feel like the system doesn't meet your fullest needs. That there's more to be than the new Soviet man. So you look elsewhere. You catch a glimpse or two of that westerner propaganda everyone keeps telling you is bad. Then you see it for yourself. Not so bad. The American way of life seems much easier and desirable. I understand Nicholas. I really do. What you must know though is that those dreams you have won't come true. Not now, and not even if we hadn't caught you. You think they were going to let you come to their country one day? Have your own house, drive your own car and spend lots of money? They were never going to own up to their end of the bargain. They used you Nicholas. You were expendable. Now here you are, facing execution or a life in prison.

"But there is a third option. An opportunity to walk away and go back to the life you had before this whole spying nonsense. Help me Nicholas. Help me catch every single one of those slithering capitalists and bring them to justice. Justice for what they did to you. What do you say?"

Naumov looked at his prisoner. He was twenty-nine, yet had aged considerably aged since he arrived. He took a sip of his tea and looked down into the cup as if hoping the answer to his predicament would surface at any moment.

"A smoke please?" Nicolas asked in a hoarse voice.

The Colonel handed it to him. He tried not to smile as the good cop routine was finally showing

111

some results.

A minute passed before Baryshnikov handed back the cigarette.

"My name is Nicholas Baryshnikov. I work as a waiter at the Leningradskaya hotel."

"You d——n idiot! Don't expect a quick ending. We shall draw this out for as long as it takes. Guard, open the door!"

***

It had taken some smooth-talking to ease the concerns of Ambassador Hartman when he'd learned a wanted man was being given refuge inside his Embassy. While not exactly thrilled, he respected the matters that pertained to the COS. His only request was that they move Torchlight out of the Embassy soon before word got out.

"You thinking what I'm thinking?" asked O'Neil once the Ambassador left the CIA Station.

"If it's something involving Technical Services, then yes," said Cooper.

"Those folks always seem to have the answer."

Just then, Chris Murray came through the vault door. An excited expression marked his face.

"One-time pad for you, from The Director himself!"

He handed the message to Carson and turned to leave. Just as he did, however, the COS looked up and stopped him.

"Chris, if this isn't the only copy, I want all the

others destroyed immediately. Understood?"

"You got it chief," he remarked, leaving to allow Cooper and O'Neil some privacy to read it to themselves.

"The President himself! As if this wasn't already interesting enough, Chief."

"Means we can't screw this up. Not one bit. First, things first, we'll need to question Torchlight more.

"I see what they're wanting to find out from him, but I think they're out of luck. He really might not know who actually is supposed to do the dirty work. Torchlight was only asked only to keep the militiamen clear of a certain section of streets here in the city. Also, he was to be given no more than twenty-four hours' notice. No, we're going to have to look elsewhere for those answers, and fast."

"I hear you," said the Deputy COS. Not exactly the best time to have agents go into overdrive when they're being rounded up out of the blue. "We know yet how they got their cover blown?

"Not a clue. I don't think we're going to be finding that out anytime soon?"

"Well, I'm going to go check on Ivanovich now and see what else he might have for us."

"Sounds good. I'll join you in a few. Something I need to take care of first."

With O'Neil gone and the station empty, Carson let out a deep sigh. This wasn't going to be easy. He was in a race against time to get the hard intel before a move was made against Gorbachev's life. On top of that, he foresaw the need to come up with a contingency plan should the President approve actions against the conspirators.

They told me this would be an easy assignment. They said all I was needed for was to mentor these young guys. Sold me a bag of goods that's what they did!

Deep down, he was thrilled to be in the thick of it for maybe the last time in his career. If this really was the last stop before reaching the end, he was going to do whatever it took to succeed at Moscow Station.

He took the DISCUS from his pocket and typed a short message to Shroud. He'd no idea if she were able to respond back immediately but he waited nonetheless. Twenty minutes later he got a reply.

Got it. Developing connection with a leading KGB General named in the list. I'll continue digging and let you know ASAP.

***

The skies were overcast as Tatiana drove outside of Moscow to General Medved's dacha. The atmosphere suited her outlook on what lay ahead. She knew the risks and feared something going wrong on an excursion like this. Curiosity and an independent streak were the driving forces though that led her to enter the bear's lair.

She slowed the car to a stop at a guardhouse on the edge of the fenced-in grounds. The guard quickly let her through after checking his list of expected guests for the day. Soon she pulled up to a large dacha with a stable and corral nearby.

"Tatiana. How was the drive?"

The General was in civilian riding attire. Walking from the stable, he carried a saddle with him.

"Your place is beautiful. How long have you lived here?"

"Ever since my promotion a couple of years back. Come, let me show you the horses," he said placing his hand on the back of her shoulder to point her in the right direction.

Inside the stable, a private was just finishing mucking one of the dozen or so stalls. The collections of horses, nearly all Arabian, would have impressed even the operators of the premier Russian breeding farm *Tersk Stud*. Beside two of the stalls were saddles made with the highest quality leather and marked with intricate designs using rubies and gold. They then came to one stall belonging to a chestnut colored three-year-old.

"She's beautiful."

"Her name's Zvezdnyy Svet. Come, I already have a saddle ready for you."

"I'm afraid I didn't bring any clothes to ride in."

"I've already seen to that. There's a room to change in over there. You'll find some ladies' riding attire in the drawer."

"You're awfully prepared," she giving him a playful glance. "Any particular reason?"

"Let's just say one never knows when an attractive woman might stop by."

Inside the small dressing room, Tatiana pulled open the chest drawer to find several pairs of riding pants, blouses and jackets folded neatly. *Just how many women did this guy entertain?* On the opposite side of the room were several pairs of riding boots of various sizes. She chose an auburn top to go along with a pair of cream-colored pants and chocolate brown boots. When she stepped back outside, the General had Starlight's reigns in hand.

"What do you think?"

"Stunning. I think it all fits you just right. Here, let me help you up."

It was all she could do not to resist his help and stick to playing dumb. Growing up on the farm back in Maryland, she had ridden almost daily from the age of five and had entered several equestrian events.

Once she was in the saddle, the General mounted a white stallion he'd named Ivan and led the way out for a ride to an open meadow. The entire time, Tatiana could sense his eyes on her. She would need to stay at least one step ahead of this one.

"Tell me Tatiana, do you often get outside of the city?"

"Not often enough. In the summer, Boris and I take the children on vacation, sometimes to our dacha in Okskiy but mostly to the Black Sea."

His face curdled in disgust at the mention of a holiday to the busy Soviet vacation spot. "Hmph. The seaside is way too crowded with all the proletariat. Here in nature is where a man can truly rest and relax."

"Boris has never been much for all the outdoors. He speaks often of fond memories as a boy in Foros.

So, we spend most of our vacations there usually."

"That's no way to raise strong Russian children. Here in the forest, one can truly reset the mind and get good exercise rather than be sedentary in a lounge chair getting fat."

Tatiana giggled. "Well, I'll give you that."

"If your husband's long lost youth wasn't a consideration, what would you choose?"

"Well, maybe a camping trip. I always had my good memories of going out in the woods with *Young Pioneers*. I guess just really exploring and going on an adventure."

The General liked how this was going so far. If he played his cards right, he just might before dinner...

"General, look over there," she said in a hushed tone. "A doe."

"Ah, you're right. Let's dismount here and see if we can't get a bit closer on foot. And call me Dmitri please."

The General dismounted and helped her down before tying the horse's reigns to a recently toppled tree trunk lying flat on the ground. They both moved slowly near where a doe appeared to be taking a drink of water by a stream. At least a mile or two beyond the stream, a quaint cabin was visible among the trees. Smoke was rising from its chimney.

They cleared all of the residents long ago to build this KGB retreat center. It's too far away from the main dacha to be for a guest. Who could possibly be there?

"Look to your left," he said softly, putting his hand

on her shoulder. She turned her head to see a small fawn playing not too far from its mother.

"Definitely don't see this at the Black Sea," she said with a gentle smile. Their eyes locked in that moment alone together. The tension was growing.

"There's so much to see," Medved said finally. "So much to be explored outside of the crowded cities."

"And away from the overstuffed politicians?"

"If I remember correctly, Tatiana Alexeev, your husband is one of them. Or at least works for one."

"I know." As she said this, she took his right arm still on her shoulder and wrapped it around her.

The General sensed the moment of opportunity. He began to go in for the kiss he so badly wanted. Right as his face was within an inch of hers, she pulled back.

"How about we go back now. Maybe you can show me around inside your dacha? The grounds and the outside look lovely, and I can only imagine indoors being even more so."

"As you wish."

What a tease, the General thought to himself. *Oh well, this little game should be over soon. The suspense will be more than worth it.*

Tatiana was likewise ready for the game to end soon. She, however, had a much different outcome in mind.

They rode back to the stables in silence. Once stopped in front of the stables, he helped her down and the two ventured inside the dacha.

"Welcome to my home."

She surveyed the hallway and adjoining rooms as a corporal took her coat. Hunting trophies and photographs from his years of service adorned the walls.

"How often do you make it out here?"

"As often as I can. Weekends mostly. It's been a bit busy lately, but I managed to squeeze today in."

"I can see why. I'd do the same."

Her shoulder brushed his as she walked in front of him towards a framed picture on the wall, her hips swaying ever so slightly—to the General's delight.

"Where was this taken?" she asked, pointing to a black-and-white photo.

"Warsaw. Many years ago. I served there at our Embassy in conjunction with the Polish government. Come, I have more to show in the study. Would you care for a drink?"

He took her hand and led her into a room covered with more framed pictures, as well as mementos of the past and several shelves of books. Tatiana noticed a small safe sitting against the wall. She also noticed the General quietly giving orders to a subordinate about not being disturbed.

"What should we drink to?" he asked as he poured two shots of vodka.

"For fresh air and majestic natural beauty: to the *Rodina*."

He handed her a shot glass and raised his. "To the *Rodina*."

After quickly downing the shot, the General went over to close the door. "My men walk up and down the halls a lot and make too much noise."

Sure.

"The Arabian was a joy to ride. Tell me, of all the horses you've ridden in your life, which has been your favorite?"

"That would be one from long ago when I was a boy. His name was Molniya. I'll show you."

He went to the safe and used a key that hung around his neck beneath his shirt. The steel door opened and The General pulled out an old photo book.

"Let's see now. Here it is. I'm six years old here with Molniya. We had him at our horse farm near where the Romanov's once had a royal stable. He and I roamed the countryside the whole day exploring and galloping about."

"Looks like he was a magnificent animal."

"He was. Shall I pour us another drink? A toast to Molniya the fair stallion?"

"Of course. I can pour them for us this time."

Tatiana went over to fix the glasses while the General continued looking at the album.

"Here you go," she said with a sensuous look in her eyes.

"Thank you. To the finest stallion ever!"

Both the General and his married female guest threw back their shot glasses as the vodka went down fast. Once finished, the two looked at each other and moved closer. The General wrapping his arms around her, gave a sloppy, ravenous kiss. Easily the worst she'd ever had. He kissed her again, and then once more. His hands were just about to wander when suddenly his whole body went limp and his head fell to her shoulder. Tatiana then took the out-cold General and placed him on a leather couch against a wall.

Match. Set. Game.

She knew that she'd have an hour before he'd awake from the unexpected slumber caused by the powder used to spike his drink. Wiping her lips with the sleeve of her blouse, Tatiana took the key the General wore around his neck and moved towards the locked safe. She turned the key into the lock with almost no effort and opened the door. *So far, so good.*

She began to rummage through the safe. Inside were other family heirlooms, as well as stacks of special issue rubles for the select few. Coming across several folders, she began to peer curiously inside them. At least one appeared to be blackmail on a colleague. Others contained sensitive paperwork he'd clearly copied in defiance of Soviet intelligence laws. Then again, though, he was a KGB General.

One last folder at the bottom. It was unmarked, yet distinct from the rest of the contents in the safe. Picking it up, Tatiana began to examine its contents. She read the first page in a hurried manner before stopping and rereading it again.

Operation Save Rodina. In order to preserve and protect both Russia and the Union of Soviet Socialist Republics, we unite behind an operational plan to eliminate one Mikhail Gorbachev and serve a warning to all ill-minded reformers...

Her mouth nearly fell open. *So this is how they plan to do it. Ambush motorcade. Several possible street intersections in Moscow including Krechni to Bolshevik and Staraya Square to Ulitsa Il'inka. The number of men needed. Munition and supplies required. It's all here.*

But what about the time of the operation? Who exactly would be carrying it out? The answers to those questions were nowhere to be found.

There was still another thing she didn't know: why was Boris's name on the list Torchlight gave to Shephard? Here, there was no mention of her husband at all.

She pulled out a Troy 58 miniature camera from her blouse and began to snap photos of the documents. Once she had what was needed, Tatiana returned the papers to the folder and put them back in the locked safe, remembering to leave everything as it was.

Tatiana had nearly left the study before remembering the General, who remained slumped over on the couch asleep. Thinking quickly, she took the bottle of vodka and poured nearly all of it out in a bathroom sink adjoining the study. What little was left she sprinkled onto his sweater. Then, carefully, she removed his riding boots and loosened his pants. He'd buy it, she thought. His ego filling in the blanks of where he blacked out.

It was on the hurried drive leaving the compound that she saw the fork in the road—one way leading back to the main highway, the other to the south, towards the lone cabin she had seen that afternoon. Maybe it was a sixth sense, she wasn't sure, but she wondered why not. Tatiana continued down the main road for another fifteen minutes before she was sure she was outside surveillance and pulled off.

They always told us at The Farm never to ignore our gut feeling. Let's see what it is.

She changed into a dark-colored jacket and a black cap to pull over her hair. Darkness began to set in fast at this northern latitude. Ideal cover for what she was about to do.

Getting out of the car, Tatiana made her way on foot through the woods, taking with her a pair of night vision binoculars. Scanning ahead, she spotted the first sign of trouble five hundred yards out. Mounted fifteen feet up on a pine was a security camera. *Which means I'll have to crawl in.* No doubt somewhere a patrol awaited her as well.

She got down on the ground and began to move through the brush, slowly thinking that there better be something up there. Thankfully Boris would most likely be late getting home from work, and the children were at a Young Pioneers meeting.

"Hey, you have a cigarette on you?"

She heard a man's voice to her right. There were two KGB Security Troops moving straight in her direction twenty yards away. Killing them wasn't an ideal option. No one could know she was here. Blending in with the brush now was her only real option.

A corporal handed the trooper with him a pack and took one as well. He pulled out his lighter and let out a long drag. "Three times a day we do these patrols. I don't get what it's for!"

"It's better not to think so much," said his comrade, a more seasoned KGB guard who had seen what being inquisitive had done to past men he'd served with. "Come, let's keep moving."

The footsteps continued her way. Closer and closer until their boots were no more than an arm's length away from Tatiana's face. She held her breath waiting for them to pass. Suddenly, her left arm, which slightly propped her up to see the KGB coming, slipped. The sound of dead leaves crackling could be heard.

"You hear that?"

"That's just a bird, you idiot. Let's go."

The sound of the two pairs of boots stomping along the twigs and dry leaves slowly faded off into the distance as they left the bush with the American illegal hiding underneath. Once the noise was no longer audible, she continued her crawl before coming to the edge of a clearing. The cabin she saw earlier that day stood nearby. Smoke continued to bellow out the chimney as lights shone through the windows.

Tatiana took the binoculars once more and trained them on the window. From where she hid behind a tree and large rock, she saw a young man close to her age cleaning an AK-47. He was not dressed in a uniform, nor were the others inside with him. She counted seven in all.

Why wouldn't they be in the barracks near the dacha? Why secluded out here all alone? Then she remembered. It was all in Operation Save Rodina: a team of seven, two drivers and five gunmen. Tatiana didn't believe in coincidences.

I've   got   to   tell   the   Chief.   ASAP.

13

The Eleventh Day

"He should be ready in a few minutes once the dosage takes full effect," remarked Dr. Pavel Vasnev as he entered the room.

"Excellent Comrade," said Colonel Naumov. "Now, we can finally break this imperialist traitor."

Nicholas Baryshnikov had willed himself not to break, no matter the trial put forth by his captors. This time though, mental toughness would be no match.

It was a drug somewhat similar to LSD, an injection that would ease one into a state of bliss. Manipulation would be fairly simple, however, not without its own risks. Permanent brain injury, and even death, had been known to occur, making it a last resort. The Doctor and the Colonel sat behind a two-way mirror with Baryshnikov on the other side.

"I will speak to him, Colonel. As we go along, please tell me what questions you would like me to ask."

The Colonel nodded. *This had better work.* His career depended on it.

"Nicholas, can you hear me?" said Dr. Vasnev into

a microphone.

Baryshnikov lay tied to a top of a table, staring at the ceiling.

"Yes. Where... am I?"

"Where do you think you are?"

"Somewhere bright and warm. A meadow, I think."

"Nicholas, you are in a forest in Northern Virginia. Your hard work has finally been rewarded and you've been exfiltrated to the United States. I'm here to debrief you for the CIA, as well as prepare arrangements for your new life here. Have you thought much about where you would like to live?"

"Okay. I would like to live in Montana. A cattle ranch just like in the western movies."

"We will make that happen then. You will love it there."

The drugged prisoner smiled. *He's ready now*, thought the Colonel.

"Nicholas, can you tell me about your work for the United States while you were in Moscow?"

"I worked as an agent for the CIA. I reported what I overheard from high ranking Kremlin officials whose tables I served in the main restaurant of the Leningradskaya Hotel for three years. I was also a courier passing along intelligence information."

"Ask him who he was reporting to," whispered the Colonel.

The doctor nodded. "That is correct. Can you tell

me some about your handler?"

Baryshnikov sighed. The two men on the other side of the glass waited for what seemed an eternity until he spoke.

"A woman. Very beautiful. Brown hair with piercing blue eyes. She would come to lunch with her girlfriends regularly. Always orders *Zefir* for dessert with black coffee. I would slip notes underneath her plate or in a napkin. She did likewise."

"Did she ever tell you her name?"

"Her name..."

The long pause made the Colonel shift restlessly. *Please stay with it, you idiot. A name even if it's an alias. Something more to go off of.*

"...I will not say."

"What?! Go in there and give him another dose now, d——it!"

"It doesn't work that way Colonel. Somewhere in his subconscious, he has locked this information away and is holding it tightly. To give him a second dose this soon would likely send him into a coma and could be fatal. Even if he didn't have adverse effects, he still wouldn't give us more."

The doctor tried a different approach instead. "That is fine, Nicholas. Could you instead tell me what you know about her background? Did you overhear any bits from her conversation with her friends?"

"Her husband...works in the Kremlin. Not sure what his job is. I believe she has two children."

Ten minutes later, the interrogation was over, and the waiter's fate was sealed. Naumov now had enough information to continue following the trail. He decided his next stop would be to visit the restaurant manager at the Leningradskaya.

***

It was late in the evening when Cooper arrived at the metro station. After an identity transfer followed by a second disguise, he stood at the platform waiting for the 9:30 to arrive. He was hoping they really were in the black this time.

Finally, the white subway train with black doors rushed forth through from the tunnel and pulled into the station. Carrying a sketchbook under his shoulder, the Chief of Station stepped aboard. The train was light on passengers at this time of day, leaving the vast majority of seats open. He took one in the back, away from the few people aboard, and began to draw in the sketchbook to pass the time.

Just before the train left the station, a woman stepped aboard. If the COS hadn't paid attention to her eyes, he wouldn't have recognized Shroud. She first sat down a few feet away, taking notice of her surroundings. There were only two passengers aboard tonight: an old woman and a man appearing to be returning home from work at a factory. Three minutes after they left the station, Tatiana moved over beside the Chief, looking interested in his artwork.

"What are you drawing?"

"Just something from a bygone memory," he said

aloud in Russian before changing his tone to a whisper. "How are you doing?"

"Spectacular. I've got some news you'll want to hear."

"Yeah?"

"Proof tying everyone on the list together."

"Allow me to sketch a drawing of you, Miss," he said aloud while moving himself to face her. He lowered his voice again. "Go on."

Tatiana told of her visit to the General as the metro train rumbled along the track. Carson listened stoically as he drew a very rough portrait of her. Finally, when she finished, he spoke again.

"You took a big risk going to his dacha and trying to set a honey trap like that. Especially with everything going on."

"A lot at stake."

"True. I won't fault you for that."

"So what now? Are we going to stop them?"

"Decision is well above both our pay grades. Here, what do you think?" He handed her the sketchbook. "You can keep it. Just tear the page from the top."

Shroud tore the paper from the book and placed it inside her coat. When she handed back the sketchbook, the microfilm rested between the pages.

"I'll let Langley know tonight. Then we'll know the next step."

"Good."

The train continued on for several more minutes before another word was spoken. The COS's mind was deep in thought. He questioned if he should continue with what he was about to say. Yet, he believed that if he didn't, this young woman could miss out on living a fuller life.

"Audrey, can I give you some advice? It's okay to think about an end game. I've seen how hard you work at this. You're persistent. You play a part so well that you blend into the scene. You've got that X factor. But there comes a time when you have to come up for air. Ten years, it takes a toll on you."

"Speaking from experience?" she said with a slight smile.

"You could say that. I guess I just see a little bit of myself in you. The very much younger self. If the tension of a job like this doesn't get you, you'll wake up one day as old as me and wonder where it all went."

"So, you regret all this?"

"No. I love what I do, but I came to a crossroads in my career at about your age and had to decide if I was going to turn a new page or continue. I at least had a wife, that I really loved, and didn't have to cut nearly all ties with my home country. After ten years, you more than have that right to decide. The Agency can make this work for you and those kids. Just think about it. Okay?"

Tatiana, or Audrey, nodded. The two identities had overlapped for much longer than she ever once imagined. Maybe it was time to start anew. Maybe, once the dust had settled on all of this. She still wasn't sure.

Ivanovich was still awake when Carson returned later that night from his rendezvous and knocked on his door.

"Hope I'm not bothering you, but I just spoke with the Deputy Director. It seems you're going to be leaving here a bit sooner than we all thought. The extraction date has been set for tomorrow at noon."

"But my family…"

"They've been taken care of. Between what you told us and our surveillance of security there, we've crafted an operation where one of our top men will be able to get them out of the apartment sight unseen. You trust us?"

"*Da*. I want to say thank you again for rescuing me off of the street near that gas station. It was getting pretty lonesome in the rundown factory. You've been a lifesaver."

Carson laughed. "I've got to hand it to you. Not a lot of guys out there who could evade the KGB like you did for as long as you did. Even as a former officer."

"It about getting in the head of whoever is leading the investigation. Think like they do and you can remain at least a step ahead."

"If you don't mind me asking, what motivated you to do all this?"

"Well, as I told my first handler years back, I—"

"I know about that already. What I mean is that there's something deeper than just frustration at a broken system, isn't there?"

Ivanovich nodded. "I've never told anyone, Mr. Cooper, but it's a pain I can't get rid of. When I lost my oldest son years ago in a senseless mission in Czechoslovakia, my whole world changed. Passing information, revealing secrets, even now stopping an assassination plot, it's all part of a way for me to strike back at a system that's taken away what once meant so much. But what about you? You look like you've been in this line of work for a long time. What's keeping you doing this?"

"Flag-waving, wanting to make a difference. Same ideals most young folks back then had, I guess. Over time, it's become much more. I know this is the Soviet Union, but are you much of a religious man?"

"Maybe bit more so than your standard atheist Party member."

"Then you might understand when I say that one day I had what you'd call a kind of Road to Damascus moment. Everything changed after that. Now, I'm in this cold war because I want people everywhere to have the ability to freely pursue a relationship with the God who saves and gives hope."

"I had uncle who led an underground church. They shot him during the purges when he refused to stop preaching about that same God who saves. If he were here, he would thank you for what you're doing"

"One day, I look forward to meeting him."

"You think of going home and finishing your

career?"

Him too? It was the subject Carson kept avoiding. He knew it was coming. Often, the COS prayed to be allowed just one more day in the field. That last day though was closer than he'd cared to admit.

"It does cross my mind some. I figure when that time comes, it'll be meant to be."

They talked for about an hour more—Torchlight drinking vodka while the Chief of Station, still on duty, sipped on his coffee. When he finally left to return to his office, Cooper thought on what they'd said.

It's closer than you realize Carson. Like it or not. When it does come, will you really be ready?

14

The Twelfth Day

Breakfast was nearly ready and on the table when Boris came into the kitchen.

"Morning," he said, kissing her on the cheek as he sat down. "Sleep well?"

Tatiana nodded as she took off her apron and handed him a full plate. "I did. Got your favorite this morning."

"*Spasibo*. Any plans for today?"

"Grocery shopping. How about yourself?"

"Oh, just a couple meetings. Outside of the Kremlin." Boris picked up the copy of *Pravda* and began to skim it for anything interesting. He could tell by the grey skies outside the window that the forecast would likely be wrong today.

"Anything special?"

"Gorbachev has an event at The Institute this afternoon at one."

An alarm went off for her at these words. She knew what intersection was near that building.

"Sounds like a full day. Which road are you taking to get there?"

"Taking *Krechni* to *Bolshevik*," said Boris with a puzzled look at the question. "Why?"

"No reason. Usually traffic around there."

"There's never any traffic for a Politburo member's entourage."

Little was said during the rest of breakfast. Boris eventually got up from the table and went into the living area to say goodbye to Sergei, who was engrossed in a TV show.

"See you tonight," he said as he rushed out the door. Tatiana didn't say a word; all she could do was feign a smile.

***

The manager of the Leningradskaya Hotel Restaurant had no idea why he was here in this windowless room. He'd awaken that morning by a loud knock at his door. When he answered, he was shocked to encounter three KGB officers saying he was being taken to Lubyanka for questioning. What it was about, he hadn't a clue. He hoped to be released soon so he could see to the opening of the restaurant for lunch.

Colonel Naumov walked into the room a quarter before 8 am.

"Please be at ease, Comrade Alskysndrov. You are not here under suspicion of anything. Rather, I require your help in answering a few questions."

"Yes, but of course, anything I can do for the *Rodina*."

"You have a group of ladies associated with the

nomenklatura that regularly dine together for lunch at your restaurant. They usually sit within your waiter Nicholas' station. One of them happens to be the wife of someone who works at the Kremlin. Could you tell me who that person is?

"There are many women who frequent our restaurant, Colonel, that have husbands working at the Kremlin. It is hard to remember exactly who."

"The woman," Naumov pointed out, "is a rather pretty young mother. Brown hair and blue eyes. Always gets *Zefir* for dessert with black coffee. Try hard to recall comrade."

"I believe you might be referring to Tatiana Aleexev. Her husband is an assistant to Mikhail Gorbachev. She has been coming to my restaurant for a long time now."

Naumov went to the door and leaned out to beckon a guard on duty. "Get me the file on Tatiana Aleexev at once."

***

The snow had stopped just as Gorbachev's entourage headed outside for the motorcade to cross the city to The Institute. Three cars would be taken, with the distinguished Politburo member riding in the front.

Boris glanced at his wristwatch. Twenty minutes to get there.

"Are we ready to go Comrade Boris?" said Mikhail Gorbachev as he stepped outside the door of the Ministry building.

"Indeed, we are General Committee Secretary."

Everyone began to file into the vehicles. A senior staff stopped as he was getting in and looked over at Boris, still standing at the curb rustling though some papers in his brief case.

"Aren't you coming?"

"Yes, however, I just realized I forgot a copy of the Secretary's speech. I shall retrieve it at once from the office and take the tailing car instead."

As the lead car passed through the walls of the Kremlin, Boris discovered his copy—placed in the wrong folder of his briefcase. He quickly hopped in the last car, and the motorcade was off.

***

General Medved skimmed through the collection of cassette tapes in his office until he came to his personal favorite: Tchaikovsky's 5th Symphony. He removed the tape from its plastic case and put it into the cassette player. As the classical melody carried throughout his office, he couldn't help but look out the window facing the east. *It won't be long now…*

The ways of old will remain as they should.

***

Nikita and Sergei both knew something was wrong. Bubbly and talkative in the mornings on the drive to school, their mother now seemed quiet with a serious disposition. Neither dared to ask what the matter was.

As soon as they exited the car, Tatiana hit the gas. She didn't stop until she found a quiet street where she could pull over. Removing the DISCUS from her pocket, she typed out a message to Cooper. Tatiana hoped he'd see it immediately. But what would he say? He could hardly get the authority in time to allow her or anyone else to interfere. Would there even be time for an answer? Pressing send, she could only wait in anticipation.

Inside her overcoat rested her Beretta M9. She had never used it in the field, much less carried it with her. Today might be that first time.

What if he doesn't see it? What then? If this guy dies and I could've stopped it, then why am I even here doing this job?

Ten minutes passed without an answer. *Screw it.* Putting the car in gear, Tatiana headed towards *Krechni* and *Bolshevik*.

***

It had taken some time to get the proper approval for the raid. Naumov convinced his superior that the trail had indeed led to the wife of a Kremlin official. No doubt the Centre's training courses and textbooks would speak of this case for years to come if he could apprehend this American woman posing as a Russian.

Naumov ordered the men under his command to hold back at the entrance to the long hallway on the apartment building's seventh floor. He casually made his way toward the Aleexev's door. Knocking loudly, he heard no answer.

"This is Colonel Naumov of the 2nd Directorate," he bellowed, knocking once more. "You're to open this door at once."

Still, there was no answer. The men now rushed

towards the door just as he motioned for them. Using a sledgehammer, one of them swung hard near the door handle for it to push open violently. The group of security officers rushed in, ready to arrest the spy. A couple of tenants cracked open their doors slightly to see what the noise was about.

"Please return to your apartments. This is a matter of state security being handled by the authorities," Naumov shouted with authority as doors quickly slammed shut. He returned his focus on the task at hand.

"No one appears to be home," reported a young officer coming from the master bedroom.

"Somebody get down to the garage and see if their car is still there!"

Naumov immediately decided to delegate the apartment search to someone else. Right now, he couldn't let this woman go.

"Colonel, a militiaman reports seeing their car make a fast turn down Techiski road."

"I want a detail zoning in on that area within a three-kilometer radius right this very minute."

***

Carson and O'Neil both thought it was a work of art. With a custom mask and disguise an OTS liaison had crafted on short notice, one would be shocked to realize the Marine officer standing before them was Pyotr Ivanovich. The fugitive spy looked in the full-length mirror in front of him and was in near disbelief at what he saw.

"I think as long as I keep my mouth shut, I should be good."

"You look as American as Springsteen singing *Born in the USA*," O'Neil chuckled. "I think it just might work. What you think, Chief?"

"Not bad at all. Hard to believe in two hours, Pytor, you'll be on that flight with your family and out of here for good. Just a bit longer."

"I'll be glad for that."

The ringing sound of the telephone came from over Carson's shoulder. He turned towards his desk and answered.

"Yeah. They did? Good to hear."

"What was that," O'Neil asked?

"Just an update. I…"

It suddenly dawned on Carson that he hadn't checked the DISCUS all morning. Unlocking his desk, he saw the message on the screen.

"Oh shoot."

"Something the matter?"

"She says her husband told her they're taking the planned route this morning. I need to get a message to the Director right this very moment."

"What time did she send it?"

"Fifteen minutes ago."

"You don't think—"

"She just might have." Cooper raced to message

her to stand down. The okay to take action had yet to be given by Langley. If she were going to take matters into her own hands, she'd be significantly outnumbered and potentially without the full backing of her government. He hit send. *Would she actually read this in the heat of the moment?* Someone had to go after her. It was breaking nearly every rule in the book, but yet, there was one lesson he'd learned that he couldn't forget: never leave your subordinates in a hopeless spot.

***

Jozef Woźniak sat shotgun in a parked Zhiguli just outside the Institute. Word had been received that the motorcade was on its way. The adrenaline was now coursing fast through his body as the moment neared. There was a very real chance, he and the others with him knew, that even if they somehow survived they may still be double-crossed and executed rather than allowed to disappear back into the shadows. To back out was not an option. Death would be the penalty for disobeying these orders.

"You remember the signal?" asked Arkady who was sitting in the driver's seat as Woz loaded a fresh magazine into his handgun.

"For Polish Solidarity, then we begin firing," said Woźniak. The shout would make for a nice scapegoat and offer political fodder for the KGB to take more decisive action against the rabble-rousers over there.

"Are you ready for this," asked another Spetsnaz commando seated in the back named Sasha?"

Woźniak looked out the window longingly. But for

a moment did he wish it all could be different. All his years' training in the KGB, going deep undercover to be activated for the impending moment. He let out a deep breath and began to put together his automatic. "I'm ready."

***

The Soviet-made sedan raced through the streets at breakneck speeds. Tatiana was taking every shortcut she knew, desperate to make it to the intersection in time.

The flashing glow of red lights atop two yellow police vehicles glared in her rearview mirror. Tatiana was unsure if it were her speeding or something entirely unrelated.

Traffic abruptly halted up ahead. She was still a block away. Making a sharp turn at the corner, she quickly pulled into a particular alley where her vehicle could remain unseen.

She changed out of her coat and into another. Tatiana then put her hair up in a ponytail and under a cap in hopes of concealing her identity. As she moved out onto the street, the two police cars passed by, the drivers not even glancing her way.

The rogue CIA officer scanned for signs of anyone watching her, but she could see no sign of a tail. She kept to a brisk walk, in calm fashion hoping to avoid notice.

The Institute was now up ahead. Its full granite exterior built before the Revolution stood out amidst the surrounding Stalin-era apartment high-rises. No cars appeared to be parked outside on the street. The motorcade had yet to arrive.

She stopped roughly a hundred yards from the building. Turning towards her left and then right, she looked about. *There out there. Somewhere. Ready to attack the next General Secretary of the Soviet Union. Maybe the one man who could change the course of history and bring hope to this desperate nation. But where?*

Parked just across from the Institute was a small Zhiguli with three men. All dressed in black, they too were waiting and looking.

Tatiana felt a chill in her blood.

There have to be others!

Nowhere was a single militia man to be found. Just as the plan had called for. It was only a matter of time before it began. She turned at the sound of approaching vehicles and saw the motorcade of four high-end cars treading along on the snow-covered ground. The fourth, however, with a grey paint job, did not resemble the other three.

***

"Now!" said the commando seated in the back.

Arkady put the stick into drive and whipped the Zhiguli out from its parallel parking spot and in front of the oncoming motorcade. Forcefully, he slammed onto the breaks and blocked the Politburo member's path to his destination.

Several cars back, a grey Volga following close behind skidded ninety degrees to the left, effectively trapping the entourage.

Two men sprang from the back doors. "For Polish

Solidarity!" they yelled as they unleashed a torrent of fire from each of the AK-47s they carried. In the Zhiguli, Woz rolled down his window and began shooting at Gorbachev's lead car. The two GRU guards seated up front were pinned down and could only hope that the protective glass windshield held up to the rain of bullets slamming against it.

***

"What is going on? Why have..." A young staff member's voice went silent as he looked out the back window of the third car and saw the two commandos jump out from the grey car. Their automatics begin firing at the thick rear window, which due to a flaw in its design, shattered almost immediately. Bullets whizzed through the vehicle. The staffer dead that instant. A security officer seated in the front heroically jumped out from the car, trying to return fire, only to meet his end speedily.

The two gunmen quickly moved up to the car, with one searching to see if anyone still lived while the other covered for him.

Inside on the floor lay Boris Aleexev. When they approached the open door, he calmly looked up at them. All had gone as planned. He did his part organizing the appearance at the Institute, setting the route for the motorcade, and alerting the conspirators once the motorcade was on its way from the Kremlin. Now, they would spare him. Maybe shoot him in the leg to make it all look convincing. His new friends would reward him when the time came.

Or so he thought.

The Spetsnaz commando remembered his orders: leave no one alive. Medved's idea to prevent unnecessary lose ends. Three shots were fired into the cabin, and the men quickly moved on.

Two cars to go.

***

Up front, the driver of Gorbachev's lead vehicle tried in vain to ram the blocking Zhiguli. The GRU guard sitting in the passenger's seat desperately began radioing for help. Woz, Arkady and their comrade hurried from the opposite side of their car and moved towards the black polished Volga. Arkady pulled from his pocket a rectangular detonator. Quickly, he moved underneath the vehicle and attached the device to the axle. Pulling the pin from it, he darted away before an explosion blasted the front part of the automobile.

Once the smoke cleared after several seconds, it was clear that the detonator had not succeeded in its intent. Built for the protection of its high-ranking passengers, the limousines for the voting Politburo members were equipped with flame-resistant gas tanks.

They would have to find another way. The driver meanwhile could be seen pulling out his overmatched Makarov pistol, preparing for a last ditch effort. He would never get the chance to use it. The three began firing more rounds into the windshield. Finally, it gave away, and both GRU guards met a fast ending. Only the privacy glass divider and the locked passenger doors protected Mikhail and Raisa Gorbachev.

Less than twenty seconds had passed since the ambush began. At that very moment, Tatiana had taken cover behind a parked car, trying to get a handle on the situation. It appeared to her that there were at least five gunmen reigning havoc on the Politburo motorcade. All had automatics compared to her semi-auto handgun. She'd need to use her head if she was to stand a chance of stopping the assassination attempt and live to tell about it.

Making a split-second decision, she began to move toward the stalled cars from behind the grey vehicle. Growing up, she'd read the legendary story of Sergeant York and his capture of nearly 200 prisoners in WWI by coming up from behind on the enemy's flanks. Now, she would use that small piece of history as inspiration.

Once she had run behind cover towards the back of the motorcade, the CIA officer took a deep breath and headed into harm's way. With a steadied hand, Tatiana took her semi-auto and fired three rounds into the closest assailant who was stepping away from the carnage left inside the third car. His body hit the pavement. None up ahead could hear the shots.

She approached the third vehicle and peered into the open door. Two dead men, one with a face nearly blown away from the gunfire, lay in the backseat. It was the one lying on his knees with shots to the chest that shocked her: Boris. Her Boris.

There was no time to process or ask why. Her fake marriage was over now and done with. That was all she could think or feel. Now, she had to focus entirely or risk the same fate in this deadly moment.

Looking ahead, she could see another gunman moving alongside the middle car in the motorcade. He fired two rounds into the vehicle, until that universal clicking sound told him that he needed to change the magazine. *Another chance to keep moving forward*, Tatiana thought to herself.

Using the open door as cover, she fired two shots at the second assailant, who slammed against the side of the car and slumped over.

Tatiana rushed up to the middle car. She could see that all inside were either dead or gravely wounded. Gorbachev, though, didn't appear to be among them. Turning her head toward the lead car, Tatiana knew she didn't have much time.

"Open the d—n door or we'll blow it off," screamed Woz. Shots rang out as he fired in vain against the bulletproof door. Inside, the Committee Secretary lay on top of his wife, bravely protecting her with his very life. It was all he could do.

"You'll need to blow the door" Arkady yelled. "Here," he said handing him a satchel. "You'll find what you need in here. I'll keep watch. Sasha, get back in the car and be ready to get us out of here fast."

There wasn't much time. Tatiana pulled the trigger twice and watched as the first bullet ricocheted off the car and struck Arkady in the shoulder. The now-wounded man appeared shocked when he looked her way and saw that a woman had shot him.

"Arkady!" Woz yelled as he saw his comrade wounded on the opposite side of the Volga.

"I'm fine," he said, motioning for him to continue

applying the putty explosive to the door handle. He then shot back at the mystery woman.

In the time between the man's amazement and returning fire, Tatiana realized she was out of ammo. *Just great.* Throwing down the gun, she quickly grabbed the second dead assailant's rifle, and inserted a new ammo magazine.

Arkady shot several rounds at Tatiana, keeping her pinned down behind the open door of the second car. She knew she desperately needed to take both men out before they blasted their way into Gorbachev's vehicle.

As the bullets whizzed by, a rush of adrenaline came over her. In the next moment, he was astounded when he saw the woman run towards him guns a-blazing.

She didn't think or feel anything. All of the training from years ago, back at the Farm, had taken over.

A spray of gunfire rained from her assault rifle, hitting Arkady in the chest. With one last effort, the man raised his gun to get off a parting shot. Tatiana knocked the gun with the butt of her rifle from his hand before hitting him square on the jaw, leaving him unconscious.

Woz was now the last standing. Stopping his work on blowing out the door, he moved toward Tatiana from outside of her peripheral view. Just as she stepped back from the gunman she'd just knocked unconscious, she felt a severe blow to the side of her head. Tatiana managed to stay alert, only to see the man readying to hit her once more and got to her feet in an instant.

She moved out of the way just in time. He then fired off a round missing her and hitting the car. Tatiana knocked the gun from his hand and kicked the man in the gut. A gasp of air left his lungs as he fell to his knees.

He was far from finished. Blocking Tatiana's next incoming blow, Woz slammed her against the car. He didn't need to know who she was or what she was doing here. All he knew was that time was slipping away before the militia arrived to intervene and put an end to this.

Tatiana tried with all her might to move into a position in which she could either apply leverage or push a pressure point and throw him back. It all seemed in vain, though, as he slammed her head repeatedly into the door.

Finally, with her last ounce of strength left she broke free and fell onto the ground, struggling to catch her breath. Woz reached for the gun lying on two feet away. As he turned to aim, Tatiana realized she couldn't get up in time to stop him.

A loud piercing noise suddenly echoed throughout the street. Then it rang again. The Spetsnaz commando looked down towards the blood dripping from his jacket. Wozniak's eyes flashed around frantically to discern where the shots were coming from.

Then, out of the clearing smoke, the answer came. It was Carson moving towards them in an unwavering stride, firing round after round into the man who threatened his officer's life.

Woźniak's body jerked several times before finally collapsing. Cooper, seeing this, now ran towards Tatiana as the driver of the Zhiguli blocking the lead car drove off quickly in a panic.

"Are you okay?" he asked as he kneeled to see if she was alright.

"I'm fine," she said as she started to stand up. As she did, Carson stood up and glanced quickly inside the vehicle through the back seat window. The Committee Secretary and his wife were a bit shaken but still alive and without a scratch.

Off in the distance, sirens began to sound. A panicked radio call from one of the now-dead drivers had reached the Kremlin Regiment, the special-unit military force tasked with securing both the Kremlin and its state officials.

"We need to go. Now!" Carson urged, taking her arm and leading her off the street in a hurry.

"Where are we going?"

"It's not safe here anymore. There's a plane ready at Sheremetyevo to fly back stateside as soon as we arrive. Come on."

"No. I can't leave. Not without Sergei and Nikita."

"We may not make it out of here as it is. There's bound to be someone watching us now." He sighed, realizing that the mother was right. "Okay, come with me. I've got a car not far from here."

15

Carson checked his watch for the third time in the last ten minutes. Parking the car just down the street from where Sergei was still in after-school activities, the COS knew they were in a race to board the plane leaving Moscow and stay one step ahead of the KGB.

"Better be quick. We haven't much time."

"Five minutes. I'll be back by then," Audrey 'Tatiana' Davis replied.

She hurried into the school to the headmaster's office and asked the secretary to call for her son.

"Is there a particular reason you have come early today, Mrs. Aleexev?" asked the woman rather pointedly. In a nation built upon routine and allergic to any sort of randomness, this secretary was very curious.

"Mr. Aleexev has been given an unexpected holiday by the Central Committee Secretary and would like for the family to spend time at our summer dacha near Okskiy."

"I will go and get him. If you will excuse me."

As the door closed and the woman went to fetch Sergei, Audrey looked up at a propaganda poster of Lenin on the wall. His eyes seemed to be glaring at her angrily, as if he would summon his secret police to have her arrested and shot immediately without even so much as a customary sham trial. Time was of the essence. No doubt, the militiamen and the KGB Regiment were scrambling to track down whoever had inserted themselves into the shootout.

Her forehead began to perspire. She figured it was just nervousness. Reaching into the breast pocket of her overcoat for a handkerchief, Audrey felt a warm dampness. When she pulled her hand back out, she saw that it was covered in blood.

Oh no, not now! She tried to wipe her hand clean on the inside of her jacket before buttoning it up one more.

Just then, the office door opened again and Sergei entered the room. The mother took the boy's hand, leading him out to the car.

"Who are you?" The boy looked at Carson sitting upfront. No one had yet thought of how they were going to explain things to the kids.

"Sergei, something has…"

"My name's Carson," he said in Russian. "Your mother has a surprise. You and your brother are going to get to fly on a military plane. How does that sound?"

"Oh boy! You mean it?"

"Yep. Now put your seatbelt on."

Shroud gave the Chief of Station an appreciative look.

***

Colonel Naumov's car had circled the block

several times when they received word that a terrorist attack had taken place just outside The Institute in what appeared to be an attempt on the life of a voting Politburo member. When they arrived on the scene, ten people were dead and four wounded to varying degrees. However, the apparently intended target, Mikhail Gorbachev, was safe. Just a bit shaken up along with his wife.

"We would have been dead if it weren't for the woman who came at the terrorists from behind," said a staff member on the second car.

"Woman?" asked Naumov. "What did she look like?"

"Tall for a woman. 5'8, 5'9. Long brown hair. Slender. Dressed in a dark brown coat with a cap. She was carrying a handgun and seemed to know how to use it."

"She fired at the attackers. Never at you or anyone else?"

"*Nyet*. She saved our lives."

"Did you see which way she ran off to?"

"She left with a much older man on foot down the street and turned out of sight."

The Colonel turned back toward his vehicle. He reached for the receiver and pressed the red side button. "This is Colonel Naumov of the 2nd Directorate. All sightings by militia surveillance of a slender brunette woman and an older man within a 3 km radius of The Institute will report in at once. Over."

He clicked off the receiver and waited for any word of a sighting. It was evident to him immediately that this was Tatiana Alexeev. What he couldn't figure out was, if this woman were an Imperialist spy, why did she come to the rescue? That thought would have to wait as an urgent call came in over the radio.

***

The Red Star Hockey Rink had developed a myriad of legends in the pantheon of Russian Hockey. From an early age, children who showed talent or came from well-connected parents would go nearly every day to the rink to hone their skill set. Many would dream, but few would reach the Soviet National team.

Nikita Aleexev had been one of the few that caught the eye of coaches and shown real promise. A starting guard for his age-eight team, he led the division in both goals and assists.

When Audrey stepped into the ice rink, practices were underway. Coming to the edge of the ice, she looked through the transparent acrylic plastic and watched her eldest son skate about the arena. It was one thing for five-year-old Sergei to leave the only country he had known. It would be another for eight-year-old Nikita. How would he adapt to a new country, a new language, and new way of life? He was close to his father. What would be his reaction to learning of his death? Would he push back when he realized what was happening? Moreover, how would he react when he learned that his mother was an American CIA officer who'd been living a lie and spying on his home country his whole life?

"Excuse me, Coach Yazov."

"Hello Tatiana Alexeev. Your son is in true form today."

"He applies himself well. He also has an outstanding coach."

"What brings you here so early? You're not usually here until the last twenty minutes or so."

"I actually need to get Nikita early. We're taking a last-second trip to the forest."

The coach bought it. "Clean air will be good for the boy. I hope you all have a good trip. I'll call him over now."

"Mother, what are you doing here early?" the boy asked as he stepped of the ice. "There's still another hour and a half of practice left."

"We're going to take a last-minute vacation. I'll explain it all in the car. Go change quickly now and don't dawdle"

"Where are we going?"

"I just said I'd tell you in the car. Now go and change out of your gear."

Ten minutes later, the race to Sheremetyevo was on. Carson drove to the airport as fast as he could with Audrey and her two sons in the car. Sergei remained excited by the last-minute trip. Nikita, however, remained quiet, still trying to understand what was going on and who this Mr. Cooper was.

Turning up the music on the radio, Carson leaned

towards Audrey and spoke in a hushed tone.

"We'll need to jump on board as soon as we pull up to the plane. Let me do the talking if we're stopped on the way there.

"Diplomatic immunity is a nice thing," remarked Audrey.

"Sometimes," he said with a gleam in his eye.

***

Five minutes after Naumov had sent out the urgent order for the whereabouts of the spy and the mystery man with her, a surveillance member reported spotting her. She had been seen walking into a nearby school and leaving soon afterward with her son, much earlier than usual.

The Colonel got back into his car and raced in that direction with a detachable siren blaring from the roof.

"Comrade Colonel," a voiced bellowed over the radio. "We spotted the car she is traveling in on Leningradskoye Highway."

"She's headed for the airport! I want Sheremetyevo closed at once."

"Comrade Colonel, we need the order given by the chief of the KGB or Andropov himself to do that."

"Then go and get it at once," he snapped. "For now, have airport security be on the lookout for anyone fitting her description. Anyone even slightly resembling her should be held for questioning and not allowed to board until I have spoken with them myself."

***

As they neared the airport grounds, Carson handed Audrey a blond wig, a pair of glasses, and a fake passport. She put them on and reviewed the passport, memorizing every detail lest they be questioned. Upon arrival, they took a turn to the right and avoided the usual entrance to the terminal. As they feared, KGB soldiers were all around, patrolling and carrying their Kalashnikov rifles.

The car made its way to a side gate leading to where their plane was parked. There, a guard stood inside a hut, checking the paperwork for those coming and going.

Carson handed over the passports for both him and one Ms. Candace Miller, as well as diplomatic paperwork showing them to be employees of the State Department. The guard looked at both passports and back at the driver and the passenger riding shotgun.

He then peered into the back of the car and saw only two luggage bags. The guard handed the paperwork back to Carson and waved them on.

Audrey let out a sigh of relief. "Almost there."

"We're not in the clear yet. Not till we take off and get outside of Soviet airspace."

The car pulled up near a VC-137 in its final preparations for takeoff. Carson got out and waved for one of the U.S. Air Force crew members to help him with the bags in the back seat.

"What did you pack in these bags? Rocks?" the airman joked.

"Something like that," shrugged Carson.

Along with the flight crew on board, a Russian officer sat in the cockpit. As was standard procedure, he was responsible for helping navigate and communicate with Soviet air traffic control, if needed. Carson could have done without him aboard.

"Anyone else?" the airman asked as he led them both towards the back of the plane.

"No, that's it. We're ready to take off." Then Carson lowered his voice to a whisper. "Are they here as well?"

"In the back," the airman muttered softly before speaking louder. "Roger that. I'll let the captain know and we'll get going."

Seconds later, the side door was shut and the plane began to taxi on the runway. Carson gave a signal to another airman, and the lights in the passenger cabin were turned off.

"Now."

Audrey and Carson then reached down to unzip both luggage bags and let out Nikita and Sergei.

"Are you both okay?" their mother asked with a mixture of concern and relief.

"I'm a fine mother," said Nikita, who had felt a bit claustrophobic in the bag but wanted to seem brave.

"Me too," Sergei replied excitedly. "Can we do it again?"

"Once is enough for today," remarked Carson. "Now you two get buckled up. We're about to take off."

"Where's Papa?" asked Nikita.

In the heat of the moment, no one had planned just what to say to them. Carson felt a sickening feeling at the question. *How do you explain that to a kid? They'll never see their dad again.*

"He's not coming," Audrey said with a somber but firm tone.

"But…"

"I'll explain it later. I promise. Go ahead and sit down now."

The continued adrenaline rush had kept her from thinking too much about Boris up until now. She dreaded the moment when she'd have to tell them.

"Mr. Cooper, it's good to see you."

Pyotr Ivanovich and his family appeared from the back of the plane. The spy's mask had been removed, revealing the face of a man who was both tense and relieved. His wife and son though were still a bit shaken up at their out-of-the-blue extraction.

"Glad to see you made it," Carson said as he shook Torchlight's hand.

"What are you doing here?" asked Ivanovich. "Is he alive?"

"Last second change of plans. Yes, Gorbachev is fine, but if we don't get out of here soon, we won't."

***

The plane made its way down to the end of the

runway to begin takeoff. Gaining speed, it pulled up and rose from the ground on a flight path headed to England. Just as it did, several cars rushed onto the tarmac. A certain KGB Colonel was too late.

"What plane just took off?" Colonel Naumov demanded.

"An American plane. It's carrying the usual officials from their State Department," replied a lieutenant managing the air tower traffic controllers.

"I want that plane turned back around at once! Do you understand lieutenant?"

"Yes, Colonel," the officer said nervously. "It will be done."

***

"Flight nine-three-seven, this is Pulkovo Center. Please turn right and set for new course one-zero-seven. Please acknowledge," said a Russian voice trying his best stab at English.

"Repeat that again Pulkovo?" asked the pilot, a grizzled major who often flew this route with Embassy officials in tow.

"Please turn right and set for new course one-zero-seven."

Though he had no idea what was particularly special about one of his passengers, the pilot was by no means going to oblige. Not even the General Secretary of the Soviet Union was going to make him turn this plane around.

"Negative, Pulkovo. This is a U.S. Air Force flight with diplomatic members aboard. We'll continue on our heading following the assigned flight path and altitude."

"You're ordered to turn back to Moscow at once," the Russian voice ordered coldly.

"No can do," he said as he clicked off the radio.

The Russian liaison, quiet during the entire exchange, was appalled.

"What are you doing? We have to go back! You heard what they said."

The Russian started to move toward the controls before the navigator pushed his shoulders down and kept him seated.

"Sit down and shut up, buddy," barked the Major. "This is my plane and I've got orders to fly to Heathrow Airport without any stops or interruptions."

In the back, meanwhile, Audrey was becoming short of breath.

"Hey, are you okay?" Carson asked, turning in his seat to notice just how pale she was.

"I'm fine. It's the adrenaline coming back down after the last couple hours."

"You sure? Let me go get you something to drink," he said as he undid his seatbelt.

"No, really... I'm..." she passed out before she could finish.

"Mama, what's wrong?" cried a scared Sergei.

Carson quickly pulled her out of the seat and

placed her on the floor flat on her back. He removed the overcoat she had yet to take off to reveal dark blood coming from an apparent bullet to the chest.

"I've got a gunshot victim needing medical attention ASAP! Somebody bring me a first-aid kit."

Both boys began to cry loudly.

"I need you two to get back."

"Is our mother going to die?" Sergei wailed.

"Not if I can help it. Now get to the front of the plane."

He reached around to feel for any signs that the bullet had exited from behind. Sure enough, there was a small exit wound on the right side of her upper back. She would need surgery as soon as the plane landed. For now, he had to stop the bleeding.

He started by taking off his jacket and applying it to both sides of the wound as he waited for help. An airman came running towards them with a first-aid kit in hand.

"How did it happen?" he asked in bewilderment.

"Shootout before we boarded. She's been bleeding for at least a couple hours now. You have any Type A blood in there?"

***

They had received the call only five minutes before from a KGB General in Moscow. Now, three MiGs were taking off from Pulkovo airfield. Their orders, while straightforward, were not accompanied with clear instructions on how to carry them out.

"Pulkovo, this is Firefox. We have the bogey on our radars 2 minutes out. Requesting orders of engagement."

"Firefox, at this time, do not fire upon bogey. Repeat, do not fire upon bogey," ordered an officer over the radio.

Intimidation appeared to be the only option available, thought Firefox. His superiors had to realize the very real consequences of shooting down a United States plane carrying diplomats.

"Flight nine-three-seven, you are ordered to turn back at once," said a forceful voice to the VC-137, different from the air controller from earlier.

Just as the pilot was about to reply with another "no can do", a light came on the dashboard, signaling an intercom from the back of the plane. He momentarily changed frequencies.

"This the pilot. Over."

"Pilot, we have a medical emergency. Let's get to Heathrow ASAP."

"Copy that. Over."

He clicked the receiver back over to the Russians. "Pulkovo, we have a medical emergency aboard and will continue on our planned route. Turning back is not an option for us. Over."

"Nine-three-seven, we would be happy to have an ambulance meet you at the airport once you land. There is no need to hesitate."

Sure thing pal

"Major, look to your left!" exclaimed the co-pilot.

The three MiGs had just made a fast pass intending to rattle their nerves. It took a lot more than a couple of young hotshot Ruskies to shake up a veteran of thirty-eight flight missions over North Vietnam, as well as a couple black operations in Laos.

"Let's hold our flight path steady," the Major ordered.

He then picked up the receiver once more and switched it to a secure frequency. One MiG stayed in front at a slightly higher altitude, while the two others moved directly behind the aircraft.

"Ramstein this is flight nine-three-seven code H1K Whisky Tango carrying State Department officials from the Soviet Embassy en route to Heathrow Airport. We are seven minutes out from international waters and have three MiGs right on our six. They have ordered us to turn around. Requesting air support to meet us three miles off Tallinn."

"Roger that nine-three-seven."

Within three minutes, several F-14 Tomcats had taken off from an air carrier that just so happened to be in the Baltic off of the coast of Sweden. There was only so much they could do. Unless the VC aircraft was fired upon, they could not engage.

***

Carson had very little medical training over his career with the Agency. Whatever he had learned was being put to use now as he raced to save his CIA officer's life.

With the assistance of the airman in the back, he was working on stitching the wound together temporarily before replenishing the lost blood.

Ten years she had sacrificed everything to take on a new identity, live on foreign soil, and spy for her country. Carson did all he could not to think about the possibility of her not making it home alive. He had to keep his composure steady. He had to keep his focus zeroed in. He had to do all that he knew how to save those kids' mother.

***

The plane now was only two minutes from the shore, but the trio of MiGs continued to keep close.

"Look! Up above!" exclaimed the VC co-pilot.

One of the MiGs was now moving to a position just above their aircraft.

"Firefox 1, you are to force them to land. No permission is given to fire on the plane at this time. Understood?" ordered the KGB officer over the radio.

"Affirmative Pulkovo," radioed back the Soviet pilot.

"Major, that MiG is descending while holding its position directly above us," the VC co-pilot observed.

"It's trying to force us down and land. Nowhere really to do that even if we wanted to. You thinking what I'm thinking?"

The co-pilot's face displayed a nervous grin. "Yep."

"Let's play chicken."

With that, the plane continued holding its present altitude while the MiG inched nearer to the top of the plane. As the two pilots locked themselves into a battle of nerves, there lay only twenty feet between their aircraft and a deadly collision.

"Thirty seconds from the coast," said the co-pilot.

The VC continued to hold steady. Meanwhile, the other two MiGs had moved in closer to apply more pressure on them.

"Pulkovo, this is Firefox 1. Target is now over the Baltic Sea. We are still within Soviet territorial waters. Requesting further orders."

The KGB officer pondered once more the consequences of shooting down the American plane. He finally shook his head and sighed. It wasn't worth a Third World War, even to apprehend a spy such as this.

"Firefox 1. Disengage and return to base," replied the officer over the radio.

Just as the MiGs began to change course and head for home, the Major looked out towards the west and saw the F-14's approaching. Out of Soviet airspace, they would now be getting a U.S. military escort the rest of the way.

***

Carson looked out the window to see the dark blue waters below. He let out a sigh of relief. *At last.*

Meanwhile, Audrey's condition had improved. They'd managed to stop the bleeding for now, with the CIA officer having regained consciousness and now talking with her boys. She would live to see her country again, raise those kids in a place where the sky was the limit, and proudly call herself Audrey Davis from Woodbine, Maryland once more.

"Sir, there's a call for you on the line near the tail," said a young technical staff sergeant.

"I'll get it." Cooper walked back and slid on a pair of headphones connected to a device picking up the secure audio communications.

"Cooper here."

"Do you have any idea what time it is here in Virginia?" a sleepy voice asked sharply.

"Excuse me?"

"No one gave you an order to have your agents play cowboy and shoot it up in the midst of some power struggle. You realize what just almost happened. When I get through..."

EPILOGUE

Langley, Virginia

William Casey looked over his notes one more time. He'd given awards and commendations often in his last four years as Director of the Central Intelligence Agency for acts of bravery or service. Nearly all were private ceremonies. This time, however, because of the highly classified nature surrounding the recipient's actions, it would take place in his office with not even family members in attendance.

"They're here now, sir. Should I send them in?" asked his secretary over the intercom.

It's time. "Okay, send them on in."

The door at the front end of his office opened as a half a dozen people entered. Deputy Director of Operations David Palmer stepped in first, followed by Carson walking alongside Audrey.

It had now been a month since their death-defying escape from Moscow. After a close call in surgery at the U.S. Air Force base in West Germany where they were redirected, Audrey was finally starting to feel like herself again. She felt a deep sense of gratitude to her Chief of Station, who had stayed by her side in the hospital and looked after both Sergei and Nikita.

Casey stood up from his desk and came forward to shake their hands. "It's good to finally meet both of you," the Director began. "It goes without saying, but you've done a great service for your country."

After the initial fiery call with Palmer on the plane, Carson was more than relieved that further investigation vindicated both his and Audrey's actions.

"Audrey Davis," Casey said as he took a small leather box from his desk. "You've gone above and beyond the call of duty in clandestine operations for your country. Over the last ten years, you took on a perilous assignment behind the Iron Curtain, putting your life at risk in order to provide vital information for the Agency. If it were not for your persistence in obtaining intel regarding the plot to assassinate Mikhail Gorbachev, as well as your swift actions on the streets of Moscow one month ago, the world might just have missed out on a chance to end this Cold War. Some initially said you were a rogue agent who broke protocol. I say you accurately read the situation in the heat of the moment. Because of this, I now have the distinct honor of awarding you the Intelligence Star."

The Director handed her the open box containing a gold medal with a star on one side and the CIA's emblem over its center. The two shook hands. Congratulations. Thank you. Not a picture was taken to immortalize the occasion.

Director Casey then turned towards Carson. The COS stood at attention, as if it were his final inspection. "Now, Mr. Cooper. You have served your country longer than few would ever imagine or guess. Forty-five years. First as part of the army intelligence division known as the Veracruz Branch, reporting directly to General Douglas MacArthur. Then, as an intelligence officer and COS for the Central Intelligence Agency. One can't imagine the sacrifices you've made for your country. So few will ever know of the missions you went on and the contributions you made. Now, I ask that you would please accept the Intelligence Medal of Merit."

Carson took the medal, one of highest honors awarded by The Agency, and shook hands with Casey as well. It was a career that was finally coming to an end. He looked at Audrey as she held the Intelligence Star in her hand, thinking about how much had changed in since that morning he arrived at Sheremetyevo International.

"I hope you'll understand," Palmer said, "but we'll need to hold on to both of those. The deep-cover operation, as well as the Gorbachev incident, must remain top-secret."

Audrey looked up at Carson and the two smiled. It was okay. Neither had entered this line of work for the publicity, nor did they desire to write a tell-all book anytime soon.

"Sir, if you don't mind me asking," Audrey spoke up, "but did we ever learn what became of the plot conspirators?"

"Despite the number of agents arrested in the recent sting operation, we still had a few in place to fill us in on that. Andropov, understandably, was furious when he learned of the assassination attempt on his favorite protégé. Loyalists at both the KGB and GRU began pointing fingers. Supposedly, arrests and executions are moving fast. About two weeks ago, General Medved appeared before the General Secretary, who you will recall was the previous KGB chairman. Disgusted, Andropov shot him himself."

"That's one old buzzard you don't want to cross," Carson remarked.

"Agreed," echoed Casey. "I think you'll be happy to know, Mr. Cooper, that Josh O'Neil has been made the new COS of Moscow Station."

"If there ever was a man qualified and deserving of it, sir," said Carson, "it's O'Neil."

"Torchlight meanwhile, along with his wife and son, seem to be adjusting remarkably well to their new lives. He personally asked us to tell you he'll always be grateful you trusted him that night at the filling station. Well, thank you both again for coming this morning. On your way out…"

"Sir, I don't mean to interrupt," his secretary said, "but you have a call from the White House on line one."

"Just one moment," Casey said to his guests as he picked up the receiver. He uttered not a word for a minute before handing it over to Audrey.

"There's one more person who would like to thank you."

"Are you serious? It can't be…" Audrey remarked in astonishment.

"Better not keep him waiting," said Carson. "Go on."

"Hello…"

"Hello, this is Ronald Reagan."

***

"So, what's next for you and the kids?"

"Figuring out a tutor for starters. Palmer sent over a list of several with the proper background checks and security credentials. It's going to take a while for them to acclimate to all of this. There's also their dad."

"I heard in the debriefing. I feel sorry for them."

"Thanks. Because it's classified, Sergei and Nikita can't ever know the truth. Only that he died serving his boss."

"Probably for the best."

"Anyway, we've got a place not far from here with the usual security detail. Nikita was able to get back on the ice at a local rink and hopefully, once his English gets better, he can start playing on a team. Sergei seems fascinated by everything here in the States. Always asking questions. I think he likes living in America."

"They're young. It may take some time, but they'll adapt and call this place home."

"You really think so?"

"Yeah, I do."

"Anyway, when they don't have me behind a desk now, they have me out at The Farm helping train the new officers."

"You like it?"

"As in no more knife's edge tension every waking moment? Yes, it's been a long time," Audrey said, smiling, "but I feel like I'm rediscovering the life I used to have—a life I'm enjoying. But what about you?"

"Me? Retirement. Find a good fishing hole, restore the old homestead, and point my rocking chair towards the west," Cooper said as he stopped in front of his car.

"You don't think you'll miss it?"

He thought for a moment on that one before answering.

"I'm ready for the next chapter. It's time to go home. Besides, can't exactly go back into the field with my cover blown now," he laughed.

"Good luck, and thank you for everything," Audrey replied. He reached out to shake her hand, but instead received a hug from the former spy.

"Take care, Audrey."

A minute later, Carson turned the ignition and pulled his Ford Bronco slowly out of the parking lot. He soon turned onto the highway and headed northeast. Singing along to a Waylon Jennings song, his thoughts drifted to his farm. *Will it still look like I remembered it?*

He finally reached the gravel road, just outside Owings, Maryland, that led to the main gate. It was even better than he recalled. Everything seemed alive and vibrant. A gentle breeze rushed through the new green leaves on the trees. He rolled down the window to let it all in.

Cooper could see the old farmhouse up ahead. The pond was just behind it. He thought about it once more. *All those operations over the years. All of those agents run, intel gathered, lives lost, close calls, fleeting triumphs—was it really worth it? Did I actually accomplish what I set out to do? Have I left behind a career and a life that mattered?*

He wrestled with these thoughts. No matter what he said to others, deep down, accepting retirement wasn't easy for Carson. The old spy's faith wouldn't let him ignore the truth, however. *Yes, it was worth it. My life has mattered. Even when I couldn't see it, God was making everything work together for my good. I've got to believe that.*

Cooper passed the gate leading up to the house. A house sitter he'd hired had been out earlier that day to make sure everything was ready for when he arrived. Pulling up in front of the white-bricked three-bedroom home, he got out and looked out over the vast Maryland landscape just as the sun began to set.

Will everything change tomorrow because of what we did on that snowy Moscow street? No. But maybe we allowed for that first domino to fall. One day, those people will be free. Free to live. Free to worship. Free to come and go as they please and be all they're meant to be. One day, we'll both, Soviet and American, no longer live in fear of a nuclear holocaust. Then there will be real peace. That, Carson, is a career that mattered.

CHIEF OF STATION

Printed in Great Britain
by Amazon